"I Didn't Ask You To Stay Here

Looming above her, everything seemed to still as he searched her eyes in a world of midnight shadows. His deep, low voice seemed to fill the room.

She drew an aimless pattern through the hair at the base of his throat.

"I know."

"Although I'm not sorry you agreed."

She matched his grin. "I'm not sorry you asked."

He dropped a tender kiss at the side of her mouth, a barely there touch that shot a fountain of star-tipped sparks through her every fiber.

"Come with me to France," he murmured against her lips.

She groaned. The temptation was huge. She'd said no and had meant it. She was starting a job Monday. She didn't want to take more charity. But those considerations didn't seem quite so solid since he'd carried her to his bed.

Dear Reader,

I'm a firm believer in the adage, *Every cloud has a silver lining.* Some horrible event reduces you to tears. You're wondering how the heck you'll ever pick yourself up and get rid of the sick, nasty feeling crouched in the pit of your gut. Then, as a direct consequence of that knock, something wonderful occurs. Something you might never have otherwise been brave enough to try or accept. Pain is transformed into hope. Into success.

When *The Billionaire's Bedside Manner* opens, the heroine, Bailey Ross, is in a bad place, emotionally and financially. She's arrived back in Australia from an overseas sabbatical that she'd hoped would be both enlightening and memorable. Instead, she'd escaped a dangerous situation in Italy by the skin of her teeth. Now she only wants to regroup…get back on her feet and repay Mama Celeca, the lady who helped her when no one else could.

Mama C's grandson, obstetrician Mateo Celeca, doesn't swallow Bailey's hard-luck story. In fact, Mateo could be convinced that Ms. Ross is an opportunist—a con, to be less polite. She's such a master that even *he* is not immune to her manipulations. That he should invite Bailey to accompany him on his annual jaunt to France is a surprise to them both. But what they discover there changes their lives—and ideas about each other and love—forever.

I hope you enjoy reading Bailey and Mateo's silver-lining story!

Best wishes,

Robyn

ROBYN GRADY

THE BILLIONAIRE'S BEDSIDE MANNER

Harlequin®

Desire

Recycling programs
for this product may
not exist in your area.

ISBN-13: 978-0-373-73105-3

THE BILLIONAIRE'S BEDSIDE MANNER

Copyright © 2011 by Robyn Grady

This edition published by arrangement with Harlequin Books S.A.

For questions and comments about the quality of this book please contact us at Customer_eCare@Harlequin.ca.

® and TM are trademarks of Harlequin Books S.A., used under license. Trademarks indicated with ® are registered in the United States Patent and Trademark Office, the Canadian Trade Marks Office and in other countries.

www.Harlequin.com

Printed in U.S.A.

Books by Robyn Grady

Desire

The Magnate's Marriage Demand #1842
For Blackmail...or Pleasure #1860
Baby Bequest #1908
Bedded by Blackmail #1950
The Billionaire's Fake Engagement #1968
Bargaining for Baby #2015
Amnesiac Ex, Unforgettable Vows #2063
The Billionaire's Bedside Manner #2092

ROBYN GRADY

was first published with Harlequin in 2007. Her books have since featured regularly on bestseller lists and at award ceremonies, including The National Readers' Choice Award, The Booksellers' Best Award, Cataromance Reviewers' Choice Award and Australia's prestigious Romantic Book of the Year Award.

Robyn lives on Queensland's beautiful Sunshine Coast with her real-life hero husband and three daughters. When she can be dragged away from tapping out her next story, Robyn visits the theater, the beach and the mall (a lot!). To keep fit she jogs (and shops) and dances with her youngest to Hannah Montana.

Robyn believes writing romance is the best job on the planet and she loves to hear from her readers. So drop by www.robyngrady.com and pass on your thoughts!

For the gorgeous Jade Pocklington
for her input on all things French!
With thanks to my editor, Shana Smith, for her
unfailing support and advice and belief in my stories.

One

"Just shout if it's a bad time to drop in."

The instant the words left her mouth, Bailey Ross watched the man she had addressed—the man she knew must be Doctor Mateo Celeca—brace his wide shoulders and spin around on his Italian, leather-clad feet. Brow furrowed, he cocked his head and studied her eyes so intently the awareness made Bailey's cheeks warm and knees go a little weak. Mama Celeca had said her obstetrician grandson was handsome, but from memory the expression "super stud" was never discussed.

When Bailey had arrived at this exclusive Sydney address moments ago, she'd hitched her battered knapsack higher as she'd studied first the luggage, set neatly by that door, then the broad back of a masculine frame standing alongside. Busy checking his high-tech security system, Mateo Celeca had no idea he'd had company. Bailey wasn't normally one to show up unannounced, but today was an exception.

Remembering manners, Mateo's bemused expression eased into a smile...genial but also guarded.

"Forgive me," he said in a deep voice that hinted at his Mediterranean ancestry. "Do we know each other?"

"Not really, no. But your grandmother should have rung. I'm Bailey Ross." She drove down a breath and thrust out her hand. But when Dr. Celeca only narrowed his gaze, as if suspecting her of some offense, Bailey's smile dropped. "Mama Celeca did phone...didn't she?"

"I received no phone call." Sterner this time, that frown returned and his informal stance squared. "Is Mama all right?"

"She's great."

"As thin as ever?"

"I wouldn't say thin. After enjoying so much of her Pandoro, I'm not so thin anymore, either."

At her grin, Mateo's cagey expression lightened. A stranger lands on your elite North Shore doorstep with a half-baked story, looking a mess after fifteen hours in the air, who wouldn't dig a little deeper? But anyone who knew Mama Celeca knew her delicious creamy layer-cake.

Looking like a sentinel guarding his palace, Mateo patiently folded his arms over the white button-down shirt shielding his impressive chest. Bailey cleared her throat and explained.

"This past year I've backpacked around Europe. I spent the last months in Italy in Mama Celeca's town. We became close."

"She's a wonderful woman."

"She's very generous," Bailey murmured, remembering Mama's final charitable act. She'd as good as saved Bailey's life. Bailey would never be able to repay her, although she was determined to try.

When a shadow dimmed the light in the doctor's intelligent dark eyes, fearing she'd said too much, Bailey hurried on.

"She made me promise that when I arrived back in Australia, first thing, I'd drop by and say hello." She stole another glance at his luggage. "Like I said…not a good time."

No use delaying her own day, either. Now that she was home, she needed to decide what her next step in life would be. An hour ago she'd suffered a setback. Vicky Jackson, the friend she'd hoped to stay with for a couple of days, was out of town. Now she couldn't go forward without first finding a place to sleep—and finding a way to pay for it.

Mateo Celeca was still studying her. A pulse in his strong jaw began to beat before his focus lowered to his luggage.

Bailey straightened. *Time to go*.

Before she could take her leave, however, the doctor interjected. "I'm going overseas myself."

"To Italy?"

"Among other places."

Bailey frowned. "Mama didn't mention it."

"This time it'll be a surprise."

When he absently rotated the platinum band of his wristwatch, Bailey took her cue and slid one foot back.

"Well, give her my love," she said. "Hope you have a great trip."

But, turning to leave, a hand on her arm pulled her up, and in more ways than one. His grip wasn't overly firm, but it was certainly hot and naturally strong. The skin on skin contact was so intense, it didn't tingle so much as shoot a bright blue flame through her blood. The sensation left her fizzing and curiously warm all over. How potent might Mateo Celeca's touch be if they kissed?

"I've been rude," he said as his hand dropped away.

"Please. Come in. I don't expect my cab for a few minutes yet."

"I really shouldn't—"

"Of course you should."

Stepping aside, he nodded at the twelve-foot-high door at the same time she caught the scent of his aftershave...subtle, woodsy. Wonderfully male. Every one of her pheromones sat up and took note. But that was only one more reason to decline his invitation. After all she'd been through—given how narrowly she'd escaped—she'd vowed to stay clear of persuasive, good-looking men.

She shook her head. "I really can't."

"Mama would have my head if she knew I turned a friend away." He pretended to frown. "You wouldn't want her to be upset with me, would you?"

Pressing her lips together, she shifted her feet and, thinking of Mama, reluctantly surrendered. "I guess not."

"Then it's settled."

But then, suddenly doubtful again, he glanced around.

"You just flew in?" He asked and she nodded. He eyed her knapsack. "And this is all your luggage?"

Giving a lame smile, she eased past. "I travel light."

His questioning look said, *very*.

Mateo watched his unexpected guest enter his spacious foyer. *Sweet,* he noted, his gaze sweeping over her long untreated fair hair. Modestly spoken. Even more modestly dressed.

Arching a brow, Mateo closed the door.

He wasn't convinced.

The seemingly unrehearsed sway of hips in low-waisted jeans, no makeup, few possessions...Bailey Ross had described his grandmother as "very generous," and it was true. In her later years Mama had become an easy touch. He didn't doubt she might have fallen for this woman's lost-kitten look and his gut—as well as past experience—said Miss Ross had taken full advantage of that.

But Mama was also huge on matchmaking. Perhaps Bailey Ross was here simply because his grandmother had thought she and her grandson might hit it off. Given how she tried to set him up with a "nice Italian girl" whenever he visited, it was more than possible.

His first instinct had been to send this woman on her way... but he was curious, and had some time to spare. His cab wasn't due for ten minutes.

Taking in her surroundings, his visitor was turning a slow three-sixty beneath the authentic French chandelier that hung from the ornately molded second-story ceiling. The crystal beads cast moving prisms of light over her face as she admired the antiques and custom-made furnishings.

"Dr. Celeca, your home is amazing." She indicated the staircase. "I can imagine Cinderella in her big gown and glass slippers floating down those stairs."

Built in multicolored marble, the extravagant flight split midway into separate channels, which led to opposite wings of the house. The design mimicked the Paris Opera House, and while the French might lay claim to the Cinderella fable, he smiled and pointed out, "No glass-slippered maidens hiding upstairs, I'm afraid."

She didn't seem surprised. "Mama mentioned you were single."

"Mentioned or repeated often?" He said with a crooked, leading grin.

"Guess it's no secret she's proud of you," Bailey admitted. "And that she'd like a great-grandchild or two."

Be that as it may, he wouldn't be tying any matrimonial knots in the foreseeable future. He'd brought enough children into the world. His profession—and France—were enough for him.

She moved to join him. Her smile sunny enough to melt an iceberg, her eyes incredibly blue, Bailey and Mateo descended a half dozen marble steps and entered the main reception room. Standing among the French chateau classic decor, pausing before the twenty-foot-high Jacobean fireplace, his guest looked sorely out of place. But, he had to admit, not in a bad way. She radiated *fresh*—even as she suppressed a traveler's weary yawn.

Was there reason to doubt her character? Had she fleeced his grandmother or was he being overly suspicious? Mama could be "very generous" in other ways, after all.

"So, what's first on the itinerary?" She asked, lowering into a settee.

"West coast of Canada." Mateo took the single saloon seat. "A group of friends who've been skiing at the same resort for years put on an annual reunion." The numbers had slowly dwindled, however. Most of the guys were married now. Some divorced. The gathering didn't have the same feel as the old days, sadly. This year he wasn't looking forward to it. "Then on to New York to catch up with some professional acquaintances," he went on. "Next it's France."

"You have friends in Paris? My parents honeymooned there. It's supposed to be a gorgeous city."

"I sponsor a charitable institution in the north."

Her eyebrows lifted as she sat back. "What kind of charity?"

"Children without homes. Without parents." To lead into what he really wanted to know—to see if she'd rise to any bait—he added, "I like to give where I can." When she bowed her head to hide a smile, a ball of unease coiled low in his stomach. With some difficulty, he kept his manner merely interested. "Have I said something funny?"

"Just that Mama always said you were a good man." Those glittering blue eyes lifted and met his again. "Not that I doubted her."

Mateo's chest tightened and he fought the urge to tug an ear or clear his throat. This woman was either a master of flattery or as nice as Mama obviously believed her to be. So which was it? Cute or on the take?

"Mama is my biggest fan as I am hers," he said easily. "Seems she's always doing someone a good turn. Helping out where she can."

"She also plays a mean game of Briscola."

He blinked. *Cards?* "Did you play for money?" He manufactured a chuckle. "She probably let you win."

A line pinched between Bailey Ross's brows. "We played because she enjoyed it."

She'd threaded her fingers around the worn denim knees of her jeans. Her bracelet was expensive, however—yellow-gold and heavy with charms. Had Mama's money helped purchase that piece duty free? If he asked Bailey straight out, what reply would she give?

As if she'd read his mind and wasn't comfortable, his guest eased to her feet. "I've held you up long enough. You don't want to miss your flight."

He stood too. She was right. She wasn't going to admit to anything and his cab would be here any minute. Seemed his curiosity with regard to Miss Ross's true nature would go unsatisfied.

"Do you have family in Sydney?" He asked as they crossed the parquet floor together and she covered another yawn.

"I was raised here."

"You'll be catching up with your parents then."

"My mother died a few years back."

"My condolences." He'd never known his mother but the

man he'd come to know as Father had passed away recently. "I'm sure your father's missed you."

But she only looked away.

Walking alongside, Mateo rolled back his shoulders. No mother. Estranged from her father. Few possessions. Hell, now *he* wanted to write her a check.

He changed the subject. "So, what are your broader plans, Miss Ross? Do you have a job here in town to return to?"

"I don't have any real concrete plans just yet."

"Perhaps more travel then?"

"There's more I'd like to see, but for now, I'm hanging around."

They stopped at the entrance. He fanned open the door, searched her flawless face and smiled. "Well, good luck."

"Same to you. Say hello to Paris for me."

As she turned to walk away, hitching that ratty knapsack higher on one slim shoulder, something thrust beneath Mateo's ribs and he took a halting step toward her. Of course, he should let it alone—should let her be on her way—but a stubborn niggling kept at him and he simply had to ask.

"Miss Ross," he called out. Looking surprised, she rotated back. He cut the distance separating them and, having danced around the question long enough, asked outright. "Did my grandmother give you money?"

Her slim nostrils flared and her eyebrows drew in. "She didn't give me money."

Relief fell through him in a warm welcomed rush. As she'd grown older, Mama had admitted many times that she wasn't overly wealthy by design; she had little use for money and therefore liked to help others where she could. There was nothing he could do to stop Mama's generosity—or gullibility as the case more often than not proved to be. But at least he could leave for his vacation knowing this particular young woman hadn't left his grandmother's house stuffing bills in her pocket.

But Bailey wasn't finished.

"Mama *loaned* me money."

As the stone swelled in his chest, Mateo could only stare. He'd been right about her from the start? She'd taken advantage of Mama like those before her. He took in her innocent looks and cringed. He wished he'd never asked.

"A…loan," he said, unconcerned that his tone was graveled. Mocking.

Her cheeks pinked up. "Don't say it like that."

"You say it's a loan," he shrugged, "it's a loan."

"I intend to pay back every cent."

"Really?" Intrigued, he crossed his arms. "And how do you intend to do that with no job, no plans?" From her reaction to his question about her father, there wouldn't be help coming from that source, either.

Her eyes hardened. "We can't all have charmed lives, Doctor."

"Don't presume to know anything about me," he said, his voice deep.

"I only know that I had no choice."

"We all have choices." *At least when we're adults.*

Her cheeks flushed more. "Then I chose escape."

He coughed out a laugh. This got better and better. "Now my grandmother was keeping you *prisoner?*"

"Not your grandmother."

His arms unraveled. Her voice held the slightest quiver. Her pupils had dilated until the blue was all but consumed by black. But she'd told him what he'd stupidly wanted to know. She'd accepted Mama's money. He didn't need or want excuses.

"Goodbye, Miss Ross." He headed inside.

"And thank you, Doctor," she called after him. "You've

killed whatever faith I had left in the male species." A pulse thudding at his temple, he angled back. Her expression was dry. Sad. *Infuriating*. "I honestly thought you were a gentleman," she finished.

"Only when in the presence of a lady."

Self-disgust hit his gut with a jolt.

"I apologize," he murmured. "That wasn't called for."

"Do you even want to know what I needed to escape?" She ground out. "Why I needed that money?"

He exhaled heavily. Fine. After that insult, he owed her one. "Why did you need the money?"

"Because of a man who wouldn't listen," she said pointedly, her gaze hot and moist. "He said we were getting married and, given the situation I was in, I *didn't* have a choice."

TWO

"You're engaged?" Mateo shook himself.

"No." In a tight voice, she added, "Not really."

"Call me old-fashioned, but I thought being betrothed was like being pregnant. You either are or you aren't."

"I...*was* engaged."

Slanting his head, he took another look. Her nose was more a button with a sprinkling of freckles but her unusual crystalline eyes were large and, as she stood her ground, her pupils dilated more, making her gaze appear even more pronounced. Or was that scared?

I didn't have a choice.

An image of the degrees decorating his office walls swam up in Mateo's mind. Time to take a more educated guess as to why Mama might have sent this woman. He set his voice at a different tone, the one he used for patients feeling uncertain.

"Bailey, are you having a baby?"

Her eyes flared, bright with indignation. *"No."*

"Are you sure? We can do tests—"

"Of *course* I'm sure."

Backing off, he held up his hands. "Okay. Fine. Given your circumstances, it seemed like a possibility."

"It really wasn't." Her voice dropped. "We didn't sleep together. Not even once."

She spun to leave, but, hurrying down the steps, she tripped on the toe of her sandal. The next second she was stumbling, keeling forward. Leaping, Mateo caught her before she went down all the way. Gripping her upper arms, he felt her shaking—from shock at almost breaking her neck? Or pique at him? Or was the trembling due to dredging up memories of this engagement business in Italy?

She was so taken aback, she didn't object when he helped her sit on a step. Lifting her chin, he set out to check that the dilation in her eyes was even, but with his palm cradling her cheek and his face so close to hers, the pad of his thumb instinctively moved to trace the sweep of her lower lip. Heat, dangerous and swift, flared low in his belly and his head angled a whisper closer.

But then she blinked. So did he. Spell broken, he cleared his throat and got to his feet while she caught her breath and gathered herself.

He might be uncertain about some things regarding Bailey Ross, but of one he was sure. The constant yawning, tripping over herself...

"You need sleep," he told her.

"I'll survive."

"No doubt you will."

But, dammit, he was having a hard time thinking of her walking off alone down that drive and Mama phoning to ask if he'd looked after her little friend who'd apparently had such a hard time in Casa Buona. Given her stumble, her jet lag, Mama would expect him to at least give Bailey time to recuperate before he truly sent her on her way. And that was the only reason he persisted. Why he asked now.

"So...who's this fiancé?"

Closing her eyes, she exhaled as if she was too tired to be defensive anymore.

"I was backpacking around Europe," she began. "By the time I got to Casa Buona, I'd run out of money. That's where I met Emilio. I picked up work at the taverna his parents own."

Mateo's muscles locked. "Emilio Conti is your fiancé?"

"Was." She quizzed his eyes. "Do you know him?"

"Casa Buona's a small town." Emilio's kind only made it feel smaller. Mateo nodded. "Go on."

Elbows finding her knees, she cupped her cheeks. "Over the weeks, Emilio and I became close. We spent a lot of time with his family. Time by ourselves. When he said he loved me, I was taken off guard. I didn't know about loving Emilio, but I'd certainly fallen in love with his parents. His sisters. They made me feel like one of the family." Her hands lowered and she brought up her legs to hug her knees. "One Saturday, in front of everyone, he proposed at the taverna. Seemed like the whole town was there, all smiling, holding their breath, waiting for my answer. I was stunned. Any words stuck like bricks in my throat. When I bowed my head, trying to figure out something tactful to do or say, someone cried out that I'd accepted. A huge cheer went up. Before I knew what had happened, Emilio slid a ring on my finger and...well...that was that."

Bailey ended by failing to smother a yawn at the same time the sound of an engine drew their attention. His ride—a yellow cab—was cruising up the drive.

"Wait here," he said, and when she opened her mouth to argue, he interrupted firmly. "One minute. Please." He crossed to the forecourt and spoke to the driver, who kept his motor idling while Mateo walked back and took a seat on the step alongside of her.

"Where do you plan to go now? Do you have anywhere to stay?"

"I'd hoped to stay with a friend for a few days but her neighbor said she's out of town. I'll get a room."

"Do you really want to waste Mama's money on a motel?"

"It's only temporary."

He studied the cab, thought of the dwindling group of guys doing their annual bachelor bash in Canada and, as Bailey pushed to her feet, made a decision.

"Come back inside."

Her look said, *you're crazy.* "You're ready to leave. The meter's running."

He eyed the driver. Best fix that.

He strode to the vehicle, left the cabbie smiling at the notes he passed over and heard the engine rev off behind him as he joined Bailey again.

Her jaw was hanging. "What did you do?"

"I'd thought about cancelling the first leg of my trip anyway. Now, inside." He tilted his head toward his still open front door.

"Flattering invitation." Her smile was thin. "But I don't do *fetch* or *roll over,* either."

Mateo's chin tucked in. She thought he was being bossy? Perhaps he was. He was used to people listening and accepting his advice. And there was a method to his madness. "You say the money Mama gave you is a loan. But you admit you have no income. No place to stay."

"I'll find something. I'm not afraid of work."

Another yawn gripped her, so consuming, she shuddered and her eyes watered.

"First you need a good rest," he told her. "I'll show you to a guest room."

Another *you're crazy* look. "I'm not staying."

"I'm not suggesting a lease, Bailey. Merely that you recharge here before you tackle a plan for tomorrow."

"No." But this time she sounded less certain.

"Mama would want you to." When she hesitated, he persisted. "A few hours rest. I won't pound on the door and get on your case."

She glared at him. "Promise?"

"On my life."

All the energy seemed to fall from her shoulders. He thought she might disarm him with a hint of that ice-melting smile, but she only nodded and grudgingly allowed him to escort her back inside.

After ascending that storybook staircase, Mateo Celeca showed her down the length of a wide paneled hallway to the entrance of a lavish room.

"The suite has an attached bath," he said as she edged in and looked around. "Make yourself at home. I'll be downstairs if you need anything."

Bailey watched the broad ledge of his shoulders roll away down the hall before she closed the heavy door and, feeling more displaced than she had in her life, gravitated toward the center of the vast room. Her own background was well to do. With a tennis court and five bedrooms, her lawyer father's house in Newport was considered grand to most. Her parents had driven fashionable cars. They'd gone on noteworthy vacations each year.

But, glancing around this lake of snowy carpet with so many matching white and gold draperies, Bailey could admit she'd never known *this* kind of opulence. Then again, who on earth needed this much? She wasn't one to covet riches.

Surely it was more important to know a sense of belonging...
of truly being where and with whom you needed to be. Despite
Emilio, irrespective of her father, one day she hoped to know
and keep that feeling.

After a long warm shower, she lay down and sleep
descended in a swift black cloud.

When she woke some hours later in the dark, her heart was
pounding with an impending sense of doom. In her dream,
she'd been back in Casa Buona, draped in a modest wedding
gown with Emilio beckoning her to join him at the end of a
long dark corridor. She shot a glance around the shadowy
unfamiliar surrounds and eased out a relieved breath. She was
in Sydney. Broke, starting over. In an obstinate near-stranger's
house.

She clapped a palm over her brow and groaned.

Mateo Celeca.

With refined movie-star looks and dark hypnotic eyes, he
did all kinds of unnerving things to her equilibrium. One
minute she was believing Mama, thinking her grandson was
some kind of prince. The next he was being a jerk, accusing
her of theft. Then, to really send her reeling, he'd offered her
a bed to shake off some of the jet lag. If she'd had anywhere
else to go—if she hadn't felt so suddenly drained—she would
never have stayed. She wasn't about to forgive or forget his
comment about her not being a lady.

She swung her legs over the edge of the bed at the same
time her stomach growled. She cast her thoughts away from
the judgmental doctor to a new priority. Food.

After slipping on her jeans, she tiptoed down that stunning
staircase and set off to find a kitchen. Inching through
someone else's broad shadow-filled halls in the middle of
the night hardly felt right but the alternative was finding a
takeout close by or dialing in. Mateo had said to make herself
at home. Surely that offer extended to a sandwich.

Soon she'd tracked down a massive room, gleaming with stainless steel and dark granite surfaces. Opening the fridge she found the interior near empty; that made sense given Mateo was meant to be on vacation. But there was a leftover roast, perhaps from his dinner earlier. A slab went between two slices of bread and, after enjoying her first mouthful, Bailey turned and discovered a series of floor-to-ceiling glass panes lining the eastern side of the attached room.

Outside, ghostly garden lights illuminated a divine courtyard where geometrically manicured hedges sectioned off individual classical statues. Beyond those panes, a scene from two thousand years ago beckoned…a passionate time when Rome dominated and emperors ruled half the world. Chewing, she hooked a glance around. No one about. Nothing to stop her. A little fresh air would be nice.

She eased back a door and moved out into the cool night, the soles of her bare feet padding over smooth sandstone paths as she wandered between hedges and those exquisite stone figures that seemed so lifelike. She was on her third bite of sandwich when a sound came from behind—a muted click that vibrated through the night and made the fine hairs on her nape stand up and quiver. Heart lodged in her throat, she angled carefully around. One of those figures was gliding toward her. Masculine. Tall. Naked from the waist up.

From behind a cloud, the full moon edged out and the definition of that outline sharpened…the captivating width of his chest, the subtle ruts of toned abs. Bailey's gaze inched higher and connected with inquiring onyx eyes as a low familiar voice rumbled out.

"You're up."

Bailey let out the breath she'd been holding.

Not a statue come to life, but Mateo Celeca standing before her, wearing nothing but a pair of long white drawstring pants. She'd been so absorbed she'd forgotten where she was, as well as the events that had brought her here. Now, in a hot rush, it all came back. Particularly how annoyingly attractive her host was, tonight, with the moonbeams playing over that hard human physique, dramatically so.

When a kernel of warmth ignited in the lowest point of her belly, Bailey swallowed and clasped her sandwich at her chest.

Mateo Celeca might be beyond hot, but, at this point in her life, she didn't care to even *think* about the opposite sex, particularly a critical one. Her only concern lay in getting back on her feet and repaying Mama as soon as possible, whether the doctor believed that or not.

"I didn't mean to wake you," she said in a surprisingly even voice that belied how churned up she felt.

"You tripped a silent alarm when you opened that door. The security company called to make sure there'd been no breach. I thought it'd be you, but I came down to check, just in case."

Bailey kicked herself. She'd seen him fiddling with a security pad when she'd arrived. Heaven knew what this place and its contents were insured for. Of course he'd have a state-of-the-art system switched on and jump when an alert went off.

"I was hungry," she explained then held up dinner. "I made a sandwich."

She wasn't sure, but in the shadows she thought he might have grinned—which was way better than a scowl. If he started on her again now, in the middle of the night, she'd simply grab her bag and find the door. But he seemed far more relaxed than this morning when he'd overreacted about the money Mama had loaned her.

"You usually enjoy a starry stroll with your midnight snack?" He asked as he sauntered nearer.

"It looked so nice out."

"It is pleasant."

He studied the topiaries and pristine hedges, and this time she was certain of the smile curving one corner of his mouth as he stretched his arms, one higher than the other, over his head. She wanted to fan herself. And she'd thought the *statues* were works of art.

"Are you a gardener?" She asked, telling herself to look away but not managing it. Bronzed muscles rippled in the moonlight whenever he moved.

"Not at all. But I appreciate the effort others put in."

"This kind of effort must be twenty-four seven."

"What about you?" He asked, meandering toward a trickling water feature displaying a god-like figure ready to sling a lightning bolt.

"No green thumbs here." Moving to join him, she tipped her head at the fountain. "Is that Zeus?" She remembered a recent movie about the Titans. "The god of war, right?"

"Zeus is the god of justice. The supreme protector. Perhaps because he could have lost his life at the very moment he entered the world."

"Really? How?" Moving to sit on the cool fountain ledge, she took another bite. She loved to hear about ancient legends.

"His father, Cronus, believed in a prophecy. He would be overthrown by his son as he had once overthrown his own father. To save her newborn, Rhea, Zeus's mother, gave him up at birth then tricked her husband into thinking a rock wrapped in swaddling clothes was the child, which Cronus promptly disposed of. He didn't know that his son, Zeus, was being reared by a nymph in Crete. When he was grown, Zeus joined forces with his other siblings to defeat the Titans, including his father."

She couldn't help but be drawn by Mateo's story, as well as the emotion simmering beneath his words. Had she imagined the shadow that had crossed his gaze when he spoke of that mother needing to give up her child?

"What happened to Zeus after the clash?" She asked.

"He ruled over Olympus as well as the mortals, and fathered many children."

"Sounds noble."

"The great majority of his offspring were conceived through adulterous affairs, I'm afraid."

Oh. "Not so good for the demigod kids."

"Not so good for any child."

Bailey studied his classic profile as he peered off into the night...the high forehead and proud, hawkish nose. She wanted to ask more. Not only about this adulterous yet protective Roman god but also about the narrator of his tale. Not that Mateo's life was any of her business. Although...

For the moment he seemed to have put aside his more paranoid feelings toward her, and this was an informal chat. In the morning she'd be well rested and on her way, so where was the harm in asking more?

Making a pretense of examining the gardens, she crossed her ankles and swung her feet out and back.

"Mama mentioned that you left Casa Buona when you were twelve."

His hesitation—a single beat—was barely enough to notice.

"My father was moving to Australia. He explained about the opportunities here. Ernesto was an accountant and wanted to look after my higher education."

"Have you lived in Sydney since?"

He nodded. "But I travel when I can."

"You must have built a lot of memories here after so long."

Who were his friends? All professionals like him? Did he have any other family Down Under?

But Mateo didn't respond. He merely looked over the gardens with those dark thoughtful eyes. From the firm set of his jaw, her host had divulged all he would tonight. Understandable. They were little more than strangers. And, despite this intimate atmosphere, they were destined to remain that way.

A statue caught Bailey's eye. After slipping off her perch, she crossed over and ran a hand across the cool stone.

"I like this one."

It was a mother, her head bowed over the baby she held. The tone conjured up memories of Bailey's own mother...how loving and devoted she'd been. Like Rhea. Both mothers had needed to leave their child, though neither woman had wanted to. If she lived to one hundred, Bailey would miss her till the day she died.

"Is this supposed to be Zeus as an infant?" She asked, her gaze on the baby now.

Mateo's deep voice came from behind. "No. More a signature to my profession, I suppose."

His profession. An obstetrician. One of the best in Australia, Mama had said, and more than once.

"How many babies have you brought into the world?" She asked, studying the soft loving smile adorning the statue's face.

When he didn't reply, she edged around and almost lost her breath. Mateo was standing close...close enough for her to inhale that undeniable masculine scent. Near enough to be drawn by its natural heady lure. As his intense gaze glittered down and searched hers, a lock of dark hair dropped over his brow and jumped in the breeze.

"...to count."

Coming to, Bailey gathered herself. He'd been speaking, but she'd only caught his last words.

"I'm sorry," she said. "To count what?"

His brows swooped together. "How many babies I've delivered. Too many to count."

Bailey withered as her cheeks heated up. How had she lost track of their conversation so completely?

But she knew how. Whether he was being polite or fiery and passionate, Mateo exuded an energy that drew her in.

Indisputable.

Unwelcome.

Heartbeat throbbing in her throat, she lowered her gaze and turned a little away. "Guess they all blur after a time."

"Not at all. Each safe delivery is an accomplishment I never take for granted."

The obvious remained unsaid. Even in this day and age, some deliveries wouldn't go as planned. No matter how skilled, every doctor suffered defeats. Just like criminal lawyers.

She remembered her parents speaking about one client her father had failed to see acquitted. The man's family had lost nearly all their possessions in a fire, and her father donated a sizable amount to get them sturdily on their feet again. She'd felt so very proud of him. But he seemed to lose those deeper feelings for compassion after her mother passed away.

As Mateo's gaze ran over the mother and child, Bailey wondered again about *his* direct family. He'd lived with his grandmother in Italy. Had come to Australia with his father. Where was his mother?

"I'm turning in," he said, rolling back one big bare shoulder. "There's a television and small library in your room if you can't get back to sleep." That dark gaze skimmed her face a final time and tingling warmth filtered over her before he rotated away. "*Sogni d'oro*, Bailey."

"*Sogni d'oro*," she replied and then smiled.

Sweet dreams.

Mateo sauntered back inside, his gait relaxed yet purposeful.

He was a difficult one to work out. So professional and together most of the time, but there was a volatile side too, one she wondered if many people saw. More was going on beneath the sophisticated exterior...deep and private things Mateo Celeca wouldn't want to divulge. And certainly not divulge to a troublesome passerby like herself. Even if they had the time to get acquainted, he'd been clear. She wasn't the kind of woman the doctor wanted to get too close to.

Bailey thought of those shoulders—those eyes—and, holding the flutter in her tummy, concurred.

She didn't need to get that close either.

Three

Early the next morning, Mateo strode out his back door and threw an annoyed glance around the hedges and their statues. Not a sign of her anywhere. Seemed Bailey Ross had flown the coop.

After knocking on her bedroom door—politely at first—thinking she must be hungry and might join him for breakfast, he'd found the room empty. The shabby knapsack vanished. No matter her consequences, she shouldn't have taken money from an elderly, obviously soft-hearted woman. Equally, she ought to have had the decency to at least stay long enough to say "thanks for the bed," and "so long."

He'd practically laughed in her face when she'd vowed to pay that "loan" back. After this disappearing act, he'd bet all he owned neither he nor Mama would hear from Miss Ross again. She was a woman without scruples. And yet, he couldn't deny it—he was attracted to her.

After her stumble yesterday, when he'd cupped, then

searched, her face, the urge to lean closer and slant his mouth over hers had been overwhelming. Last night while they'd spoken among the shadows of these gardens, he'd fought to keep a lid on that same impulse. Something deep and strong reacted whenever she was near. Something primordial and potentially dangerous.

He'd felt this kind of intense chemistry once before, Mateo recalled, looking over the statue of mother and child Bailey had found so interesting last night. Unfortunately, at twenty-three he'd been too wet behind the ears to see that particular woman for what she was: a beautiful, seductive leech. He'd fallen hard and had given Linda Webb everything she'd wanted. Or, rather, he'd *tried*. Expensive perfume, jewelry, even a car. She was an unquenchable well. Took twelve months and a ransacked savings account before he'd faced facts—unemployed Linda hadn't wanted a fiancé as much as a financier.

Unlike Mama, he had no problem with being wealthy. He'd worked hard to achieve this level of security and he wouldn't apologize for doing well. He also liked to be generous—but only where and when his gifts were put to good use and appreciated. That cancelled out the likes of Linda Webb and Bailey Ross.

Giving up the search, Mateo rotated away from a view of bordering pines at the same time he saw her.

Beyond the glass-paneled pool fence, a lithe figure lay on a sun lounge, floppy straw hat covering the back of her head and the teeniest of micro bikinis covering not much of the rest. An invisible band around Mateo's chest tightened while his clamoring heartbeat ratcheted up another notch. Last night in the moonlight she'd looked beyond tempting, but in an almost innocent way. There was nothing innocent about the way Miss Ross looked this morning.

Those bikini bottoms weren't technically a thong, but

far more was revealed by that sliver of bright pink fabric than was covered. Minus the jeans, her legs appeared even longer, naturally tanned. Smooth. His fingertips, and other extremities, tingled and grew warm. He couldn't deny that every male cell in his body wanted to reach out and touch her.

One of Bailey's tanned arms braced as she shifted on the lounge. The disturbed floppy hat fell to the ground. When she blindly felt around but couldn't find it, she shifted again, pushing up on both palms. A frown pinched her brow and, as if she'd sensed him standing nearby, her gaze tipped higher then wandered across the lawn.

When their eyes connected, hers popped and she sprang up to a sit while Mateo fought every impulse known to man to check out the twin pink triangles almost covering her perfect breasts. With difficulty, he forced his face into an unaffected mask.

Get a grip. You're a medical doctor. An obstetrician who has tended hundreds of clients.

But there was a distinction between "work" and this vastly different environment. Irrespective of profession, he was still a man, complete with a man's urges and desires. Under normal circumstances, being physically attracted to a member of the opposite sex was nothing immoral. Trouble was…he didn't *want* to be attracted to Bailey Ross. Whether she was a victim or a schemer, she was a drifter who seemed to court trouble.

As Bailey swiped her T-shirt off the back of the lounge, Mateo set his hands in his trouser pockets and cast an aimless glance around. When he was certain her top half was covered, he crossed over.

"I took an early morning dip," she said as he entered the pool area.

"When I couldn't find you inside, I thought you'd run off."

She frowned. "I wouldn't leave without saying goodbye."

"Unless I was your fiancé?"

"I'm grateful for the bed," she said, standing, "but not appreciative enough to listen to any more of your put-downs."

He moved to the rock waterfall, wedged his hands in his pockets again and, after debating with himself several moments, said calmly, "So tell me more about your situation."

"So you can scoff?"

"So I can understand."

Dammit, one minute he was wanting to help, offering her a bed, the next he was lumping her in the same class as Linda. Was Bailey genuine about paying that money back, or were her dealings with Mama merely a side issue for him? Was his interest more about that long fair hair, those blazing blue eyes?

That, after his last comment, seemed to have lost a little of their fire.

Folding back down again, she set that straw hat on her lap and explained.

"After that night...the night Emilio proposed," she said, "his sisters jumped into organizing the wedding. Emilio set the date two months from the day he shoved that ring on my finger. He wouldn't listen when I told him it was a mistake. He only smiled and tried to hug me when I said this had all happened too fast. Everyone kept saying what a great catch he was."

"Not in your opinion."

"Sure, we had fun," she admitted. "Up to that point. But after that night, whenever I got vocal and tried to return his ring, Emilio got upset. His face would turn red and beads of sweat would break on his brow. He'd proposed, he'd say, and I'd accepted. I'd taken his family's charity by working at the taverna and sleeping under their roof. We were getting married and he knew once I got over my nerves I'd be happy. I didn't have nearly enough money for a ticket home. I was trapped." Looking at her feet, she exhaled. "One day at Mama's place, I broke down. We were alone and when she asked what was wrong I told her I couldn't go through with the wedding. Everyone else might have been in love with Emilio but I wasn't."

"Why not call your father?"

Regardless of disagreements, family was family. His own father had been there through thick and thin. Or rather the man he knew as a father was.

"If I introduced you to Dad," she plopped her hat back on her head, "you'd understand why. I went overseas against his advice. The last thing he said to me was that if I was old enough not to listen, I was old enough to figure out my own problems." Her voice dropped. "Believe me, he wouldn't want to know."

"You've made a few mistakes in the past?" An insensitive question, perhaps, but he was determined to get to the bottom of this maze.

"Nothing monumental."

"Until this."

Screwing her eyes shut, she groaned. "I knew I could've said no to Emilio on the day of the wedding, but I couldn't bear to think of everyone's meltdown, particularly his. Or I could simply have packed up and stolen off in the middle of the night and moved on to the next town. But Emilio proved to me he wasn't the kind to let go what he believed was his. He'd come after me and do all he could to bring me back."

From what Mateo remembered of Emilio, he had to agree. Beneath the superficial charm lived a Neanderthal.

Moving to a garden crowded with spiky Pandanus palms, Mateo swept his foot to move stray white pebbles back into their proper bed.

"What makes you so sure he won't come here?"

"I'm *not* sure. I mailed him a package from the airport. The letter explained how I wished he'd listened and I wasn't coming back. I put his ring in, as well. Hopefully that will be enough."

Mateo grunted. "He's thick but not entirely stupid." When she glanced over, curious, he explained. "The summer before I left Italy, a twelve-year-old Emilio tried to call me out. Can't recall the reason now but certainly nothing to warrant a fistfight. When Emilio and a couple of friends cut me off in an alley, I defended myself. Emilio didn't bother me after that."

Surrounded by memories, Mateo absently brushed more pebbles into the garden bed. How different his life would have been if he'd stayed in Casa Buona. What if no one had come for him all those years ago in France? What would have become of him then? If Mama hadn't offered her help to this woman—if what she said was true—what would have happened to Bailey?

"I'm going to pay her back," Bailey insisted. "If it takes five years—"

"Mama may not *have* five years."

Her head went back as if she hadn't considered Mama's advanced age. But then one slender shoulder hitched up and she amended. "I'll get a loan."

A loan to pay a loan. "With no job?"

Sitting straighter, she crossed those long tanned legs. "I'm fixing that."

"Looks like it," he muttered, eyeing the pool sparkling with golden east coast sunshine. Linda was always on the verge of getting a job too.

Bailey's jaw tightened. "Accepting Mama's money wasn't any moral highlight—"

"And yet you did accept."

The frustration in her eyes hardened before the irritation evaporated into resignation. She slowly shook her head. "Someone like you...you could never understand what it's like to feel powerless."

Oh, but he *did* know. And he'd spent his entire adult life making certain he never felt powerless again. He'd done it through hard work, not lying around a pool. Although part of her plan had merit.

"Getting a loan is a good idea," he said, "but not from an institution. There's interest. If you get behind, there are fees."

"Maybe I should throw some cash at a roulette wheel," she groaned.

"I have a better idea. I'll pay Mama the money you owe—"

"What?" She shook her head. "Absolutely not!"

"—and you can pay me back."

"I don't want to owe *you* anything."

"So you're not serious about paying her back as soon as possible?"

She eyed him as Little Red Riding Hood might eye the big bad wolf.

"What are the terms?" She finally asked.

"A signed agreement. Regular repayments."

"Why would you do that for me?"

"Not for you. For my grandmother." The amount Bailey owed wouldn't make a dent in any of his accounts but he liked to think that, for once, Mama wouldn't be left out of pocket by virtue of her soft heart.

Bailey pushed to her feet, paced around the back of the sun lounge, studied him and then, defiant, crossed her arms. A few more seconds wound out before she announced, "Well, then, I'd better get cracking."

That floppy hat stuck on her head, she fished her jeans out of her knapsack and drove her legs through the denim pipes. When he realized he'd been staring while she wiggled and scooped her bottom into the seat of her jeans, he jerked his gaze away and heard her zip up. He'd already faced the fact Miss Ross wasn't the kind of woman with whom he wished to become more involved than he already was.

In time, he looked back to see her heading for the pool gate, that knapsack swinging over a shoulder. "Where are you going?"

"To get a job. I'll be back by five to sign that contract. And about those repayments..." She stopped at the gate and her glittering blue eyes meshed with his. "I want them as steep as possible."

His eyebrows jumped. "To get the debt paid off in record time?"

"To get you out of my life ASAP."

As she strode away, Mateo gave himself permission to drink in the sway of those slim hips and long hair. High on each thigh, his muscles hardened as his thoughts gave over to how those curves and silk might feel beneath his fingers, his lips....

Regardless of whether she took Mama's money or not, she was attractive and fiery and...something more. Something he would dearly love to sample.

Whether it was good for him or not.

Four

Bailey visited every employment agency she could find, unfortunately with little success. Although initially there seemed to be some prospects, they turned out to be either charity work or commission-based jobs, like knocking on doors.

Time and again she'd been asked about qualifications. No high school diploma. One year of an apprenticeship at a hair salon. She'd been a school crossing guard, helping kids cross streets for a while. Mainly she'd performed waitress work.

She'd been directed to a hospitality recruitment agency. Placements were available at exclusive establishments but she didn't have the experience necessary to be put forward as a candidate. Many courses to enhance her skills, however, were available. But they cost money and Bailey didn't have the time to spare. She needed to start earning. Needed to start paying back and showing Mateo Celeca she wasn't a con artist but merely someone who'd needed a hand up.

As weary as she felt after a full day trekking around the city, she tried to keep her spirits high. Her mother had always said there was good in every situation. Bailey didn't quite believe that; what was so good about having a stroke take a parent out at age thirty-five? But Bailey did believe in never giving up. Her mother would have wanted her to stay strong and believe in herself, even now when she'd never felt more alone.

In the busy city center, with traffic and pedestrians grinding by, she'd pulled out her bus timetable and had found a suitable link when a familiar voice drew her ear. Masculine. Tense. The tone sent simultaneous chills and familiar warmth racing over her skin. She hadn't heard that voice in over a year. Back then it had told her not to come home begging.

Her heart beating high in her throat, Bailey looked carefully over her shoulder. Her father stood on the curb, phone pressed to his ear, announcing his displeasure over a jury verdict gone wrong.

In an instant, Bailey couldn't draw enough breath. She had the bizarre urge to run—both toward her father and away from him. Never would she have simply waltzed up to his door and thrown out her arms, and yet now—with him available such a short distance away—she couldn't help but relive those much earlier days…times when her dad had taken her horseback riding, or suffered answering inane questions from an eight-year-old while he worked on depositions. When she'd come down with tonsillitis he'd rushed her to the doctor. He'd even taken time off to nurse her back, complete with spoon-fed antibiotics.

And that was a full year after her mother had died.

Bailey's throat convulsed at the same time her eyes misted over.

He was right there.

A now-or-never feeling fell through her middle as she

moved one foot forward, and another. Maybe he hadn't meant to sound so harsh. So final. Maybe he *wouldn't* turn her away. She was his only child, after all. Perhaps he'd cry out in surprise and wrap his arms around her. Tell her that he'd missed her and ask that she come home with him now. Straight away.

An uncertain smile quivering on her lips, she'd cut the distance separating them by half when a cab swung into the curb. Before Bailey could think to call out, Damon Ross had flung open the door and, phone still at his ear, slid into the backseat. Her hand was in the air, a single word on her tongue, when the cab cut into a break in traffic and shot away.

Her hand lowered and stomach dropped. Blinking furiously, she fought back the bite of rising tears and disappointment. But, no matter how much it hurt, that bad timing was probably best. The cab swerving in at that exact moment had saved her from herself. Her father had said she'd regret dropping out of school and while that was one thing he'd been right about, there was a whole lot more that had never needed to be said. But it was too late for those kind of regrets. Nothing could be done about the past.

Determined, Bailey walked a straight line to the bus stop.

Now the future was all that mattered.

She'd told him five, but Bailey didn't get back to Mateo's mansion until six. Answering the bell, he threw open the door, took in her appearance and frowned. Bailey drew herself up, entered the foyer and fought the impulse to ease the sandals off her feet, grimy with city dirt. God, she must look like an urchin in need of a warm meal and a bath.

He closed the door. "No luck on the job front?"

"There are a few possibilities." She firmed the line of her mouth and almost succeeded in squaring her shoulders. "I'll be out again tomorrow. I just wanted to let you know I haven't skipped town. I have every intention of going through with my end of the deal." Taking up his offer of a loan and signing a contract that would legally commit her to paying every penny back, the sooner the better. She wanted this episode of her life over as much as Mateo must, too.

But then she stopped to take in his attire—custom-made trousers and a black jersey knit shirt that covered his shoulders and chest like a dream. His scent was hot and mouth-wateringly fresh. His shoes were mirror polished.

"Are you on your way out?"

Seemed she was destined to show up on his doorstep whenever he was about to head off.

"I spoke with a friend today," he said. "We went to university together. I delivered his baby boy."

"Having an obstetrician friend must come in handy."

He conceded a smile. "Alex's wife worked in real estate," he went on in that rich deep voice that resonated like symphony base chords through the foyer. "Rental properties. Natalie still works a couple of days a week to keep her hand in."

"Smart lady."

And you're telling me all this...why?

As if reading her thoughts, he explained. "Since my trip's been delayed, I suggested we catch up for dinner. Alex thought you might like to come."

At the same time a muscle in his jaw flexed, a wave of anticipation, and apprehension, rippled between them and Bailey fought the urge to clear her ears.

"Your friend doesn't know me. You barely know me and, call me paranoid, but I have the impression you don't like me much."

His closest shoulder hitched and dropped. "We have to eat." She narrowed her eyes at him. Since when had "he" and "she" become "we"? "Unless you have other plans," he finished.

Her only other plans entailed checking into an affordable hotel. The more interesting question was, "How did you explain me to your friend?"

"I told him the truth."

"That I took money from your grandmother and you don't mean to let me out of your sight until I've paid back every cent?"

"I said you were a friend of Mama's returned to Australia."

Bailey held that breath. His expression was open. Given she'd kept her word and come back today, were his suspicions about her character being unfavorable starting to wane? Not that his opinion of her should matter...only, if she were completely honest, for some reason they did.

He thrust his hands in his trouser pockets. "Of course, if you're not hungry—"

"*No*. I mean, I *am*." In fact, now that food had been mentioned, her empty stomach was reminding her she hadn't eaten since a muffin several hours earlier. But...wincing, she looked down and felt the day's dust on her skin. "I'll need a shower."

"Table's not booked till seven-thirty."

Bailey nibbled her lower lip. There was something else. Something any female would be reluctant to admit. "I, um, don't have another dress." From the look of Mateo's crisp attire, jeans and a T-shirt wouldn't cut it.

When his gaze skimmed her frame, her eyes widened. She'd felt that visual stroke like a warm slow touch.

He gave a sexy slanted grin. "What you're wearing," he said, "will be fine."

Twenty minutes later, showered and somewhat refreshed, Bailey followed Mateo to the garage. She was determined not to drink in the way the impression of his shoulder blades rolled beneath that black shirt or recall how delectable that back had looked so bronzed and bare in the moonlight last night.

As much as she'd like to, she couldn't deny she was physically attracted to the man. That didn't mean she should dwell on bone-melting images of him as she had done while standing beneath the showerhead mere moments ago. She hadn't been able to pry her thoughts from memories of Mateo strolling among those lifelike statues. Worse, she couldn't help but speculate on how those strong toned arms might feel surrounding and gathering her in, or how the bow of his full lower lip might taste grazing languidly back and forth over hers....

Now another image faded up in her mind—Mateo Celeca, gloriously naked and poised above her in that beautiful big upstairs bed. Her throat immediately thickened and beneath her bodice, nipples peaked and hardened. Slowing her step, Bailey pushed out a breath. She might have been engaged to Emilio but he'd never affected her this way. No man had. Why should that be so when, not only had she and Mateo locked horns, they'd only known each other a day?

In the garage, he showed her to the passenger side door of an expensive low-slung vehicle. A Maserati, if she wasn't mistaken. Odd there wasn't at least one or two other sports cars housed in the overly spacious garage. Or, perhaps, something classier to more aptly suit his station, like a Bentley or Rolls.

The garage door whirred up and soon they were cruising down the tree-lined drive and out on to a quiet street bordered by wide immaculate sidewalks where women in designer tracksuits walked poodles showing off diamanté collars. These people couldn't have the foggiest idea how the other half lived.

"I phoned someone else today," Mateo said, changing gears.

"Mama?" She guessed, and he nodded. "I wanted to be half settled before I called or wrote her."

"She figured that."

"Did you tell her that you invited me to stay last night?" She asked, feeling a little awkward over it. Not that Mama would mind in the least.

"I told her you rested at my house overnight and you were out looking for a job." Large sure hands on the steering wheel navigated a corner. "She said you should stay until you were earning and set up some place."

Closing her eyes, Bailey groaned as her cheeks grew hot. Mama was a lovely lady. She was only showing that she cared. But, "I'm sure you told her I'd be fine."

"I said I'd offer."

"You *what?*"

"I said you could stay for a couple of days until things were sorted out."

Bailey thought that statement through. "You mean things like our loan agreement?"

He gave an affirmative grunt. "And it's not as if the house isn't big enough to accommodate one more." He skated over a defining look. "For a few days."

Before she could argue, he turned the conversation toward the couple they'd be dining with that night—Natalie and Alex Ramirez. But Bailey's thoughts were stuck on Mateo's offer to stay in his home. She didn't want to sponge. But a few days grace to set herself up would be heaven-sent. She was willing to work at anything to get her life back on track, and quickly. Surely a job would turn up in the next day or two.

When they pulled up at a well-to-do address, Bailey's stomach flipped. She shouldn't be surprised that the Ramirez abode almost rivaled Mateo's in size and grandeur. Of course his friends would be wealthy. But beyond that, despite her nerves, she was curious to meet people the doctor liked to spend time with and perhaps learn a little more about the enigma that was Mateo Celeca. She only wished she was dressed more appropriately, and that she had a better pair of shoes to wear out. Dinner with this type meant more than pulling up a chair in a pizza joint.

Mateo slid out of the car. When he opened her door, she accepted his hand and a flurry of sparks shot like a line of lit gunpowder up her arm. Easing out into the forecourt, although her heart was thumping, Bailey managed to keep her expression unaffected. She'd felt this buzz before, when he'd caught her yesterday and, holding her chin, had looked into her eyes. Tonight the effect was even more pronounced. If an everyday act like hands touching caused this kind of physical reaction, she couldn't fathom how something of consequence might affect her…like a no-holds-barred penetrating kiss.

Did Mateo feel it too?

A stunning brunette holding a young child dressed in a blue jumpsuit, and a tall, dark-haired man answered the door. At the same time the man—Alex Ramirez—stepped aside to show his guests through, his wife put out her free hand. Her nails were French tipped. The princess-cut diamond solitaire was enormous. "You must be Bailey. I'm Natalie and this little fellow is Reece." She bounced the baby and he smiled and squealed again. "Come in, and bring that handsome devil with you."

Mateo leaned in to brush a light kiss on Natalie's cheek before shaking his friend's hand heartily then returning close to her side again, as if he could sense her anxiety. As if they might be a genuine couple.

As they all moved into a sumptuous living room, furnished with contemporary leathers and teak, Bailey took in Natalie's exquisite dress. Cut just below the knee, the lilac fabric shimmered beneath strategically placed downlights. The effect was dazzling, bringing out her complexion and intensity of her long dark hair. Her shoes matched the dress, lilac, delicate heels. Her toenails were painted red. Had she enjoyed a professional pedicure earlier that day?

Glancing down, Bailey cringed.

Her own toes hadn't seen a lick of polish in too long to remember.

Everything in Casa Buona had been so relaxed. She hadn't needed much, although, in order to travel light—to leave quickly when she had—she'd left a number of pretty skirts and tops behind, casual bright wear that suited work at the taverna. Despite the way it had all ended, she'd enjoyed being part of the staff there, serving tables, joining in on the songs and chatter afterward when the kitchen had closed for the night.

How would *this* evening end? With brandy and cigars in the study for the men, most likely. Perhaps flutes filled with Cristal offered to the ladies. And when Mateo drove her home...

Standing beside the liquor cabinet, Alex rubbed his hands together. "What can I offer you to drink?"

"I'm fine," Bailey replied, "thank you." Given her inquisitive thoughts regarding Mateo, better she stayed well clear of beverages that would only weaken inhibitions.

"Ice water for me, Alex," Mateo said, moving to stand alongside her, close enough to soak in the natural heat emanating from his body. "You and Natalie can indulge a little tonight."

"It's true." Natalie rubbed her nose with her baby's. "It isn't often we get a night off."

The little boy giggled and held his mother's cheeks. When his fingers caught in her perfectly coiffed hair, Natalie only laughed, but then worried over a strand wrapped around one tiny finger. Alex walked over, unwound the hair from around his boy's finger then kissed the baby's palm with a loud raspberry that sent the child into peals of laughter.

Bailey's chest squeezed. This trio was the picture of the perfect family. The happiness they so obviously shared lit all their faces. What they had couldn't be bought.

That's what *she* wanted one day. The kind of marriage that took a person's breath away. The kind of love her parents had once shared. They'd been so happy. When she was young, she'd never stopped to think it might not last.

When she refocused, a feathery feeling brushed over her. She looked across. Mateo was looking at her, a curious light shining in those dark eyes, a sexy grin curving one side of his mouth. A pulse in Bailey's throat began to beat fast. She blinked then, uncertain of where to look, concentrated on Alex who sent her an ambiguous smile before returning to the bar to see to the drinks.

Natalie spoke to her husband as he poured a water then what looked like scotch for himself.

"Honey, I might change his diaper for Tammy before we go." Natalie explained to Bailey, "Tammy's the wonderful lady who looks after Reece when I go into the office a couple of times a week. She's catching up on her knitting in the family room until we leave."

"Mateo mentioned that you work outside of the home."

"It's a great balance. Only four hours each day—" Natalie rubbed noses with her baby again "—and then I'm dying to get back to him." She met Bailey's gaze. "Want to help me change him?"

Bailey's knees locked. She'd done some babysitting but never one so young. "I'm not sure I'd be any help."

Natalie only smiled. "You look like a quick study."

They left the men, who were busy discussing football, and moved into a nearby room—a downstairs nursery. Bouncing the baby, Natalie crossed to a white lacquered changing table where she gently lay her bundle down then set about unbuttoning his suit.

"Mateo mentioned you know Mama Celeca?"

"I lived in her town for a few months."

"I've heard so much about her. Alex says she's the biggest darling ever. He went with Mateo to Italy one summer a long time ago. Apparently Mama tried her best to get both of them married off."

She seemed so genuine, Bailey couldn't help but like her. Couldn't help but feel relaxed and at home, even in a dress that looked more like a rag next to Natalie's exquisite creation.

Bailey brushed a palm over the baby's soft crown and carried on the thread of their conversation.

"Lucky for you Mama's matchmaking didn't succeed."

"Lucky isn't the word." Natalie peeled back the diaper and let out a pleased sigh. "I love when there's no messy surprises. Could you hand me a fresh diaper, please?" Natalie cast a glance to her right. "They're in that lower drawer."

Bailey dug one out while Natalie cleaned up, shook on powder then slid the fresh diaper under the baby's bottom.

"Mateo mentioned that you're in between jobs," Natalie said, pressing down the diaper tabs.

"I was out looking today." *All* day.

"Find anything?"

"Not yet."

Natalie took both the baby's feet and clapped the soles together, but the baby's smile was a little slow to bloom this time. Must be past his bedtime, Bailey thought.

"What are you interested in?" Natalie asked, scooping her baby up. "Do you have office skills?"

"Afraid not. I've been waitressing, serving and general cleanup."

"In Italy?" Bailey nodded and Natalie beamed. "What an adventure."

Bailey arched a brow. "It certainly was that."

"I don't know of any waitressing positions, but we're always after good cleaners for rentals at the agency."

Bailey's heart leapt. "Really?"

With the baby's head resting against her shoulder, Natalie headed for the door. "You're probably not interested—"

"No," Bailey jumped in. "I mean, *yes*. I *am* interested. When do you think I could start?"

"I'm going in Monday. I'll give you the address."

"I'd appreciate that." A *lot*. "Thank you."

Natalie's pace had slowed. The baby's eyelids were drooping now. He was about to drift off. "Would you like a cuddle before we leave?"

Bailey gave a nervous laugh. She would. He was so adorable and full of smiles. But what if she took him and he cried? She'd feel terrible. But, as if to reassure her, little Reece stretched his arms out to her and found a drowsy smile.

"Seems at least one of you wants a cuddle," Natalie joked. But then she saw Bailey's hesitation. "He's a darling, honest. The worst he'll do is pull your nose."

Bailey blew out a shaky breath. "Well, I've never had my nose pulled before." She put out her arms.

The baby weighed more than she thought. Close up, his heavy-lidded eyes looked even bluer. And he smelled divine— all fresh and new. No wonder Natalie and Alex were so happy. They had it all.

"He likes your bracelet." Natalie touched the dangling charms that Reece was fingering too. "So do I. Did you get it overseas?"

"It was a gift." And then Bailey admitted what she hadn't in a very long while. "A gift from my mother."

"Then it's doubly precious. Do your parents live in Sydney?"

"My father does. My mother passed away."

Natalie's beautiful face fell. "Oh…I'm so sorry, Bailey."

"It was a long time ago."

The sudden lump in Bailey's throat made speaking a little difficult. Over a decade had passed since her mother's death. Not everyone would understand why her grief hadn't faded. But something about Natalie made Bailey feel as if she would. As if the two of them could be more than acquaintances. That, maybe, they could be friends.

Still, she didn't want to mire down the conversation, not when Reece was mumbling adorable things she couldn't quite understand and hiccuping in such a cute way.

But Natalie's expression had grown alarmed. Slanting her head, she held out her arms.

"I think you'd better give him back."

Bailey's heart sank. "Did I do something wrong?"

"No, no. It's just I think he's about to—"

Natalie didn't move quickly enough. Reece gave another hiccup. Heaved a little. Then a lot. Next his dinner came up.

All over the front of Bailey's dress.

Five

When Natalie barged into the room, Mateo and Alex had been discussing the state's current public hospital concerns. Mateo immediately dropped the conversation and peered past Natalie's shoulder. Bailey wasn't in tow and Natalie's hands were clasped tight before her. Seemed unlikely—Natalie was one of the sweetest people he knew. But Bailey was a relatively unknown quantity. Had the women had a disagreement?

Natalie pulled up in front of her husband. "Can you ring and let the restaurant know we'll be late?"

Standing, Alex caught her arm. "Is the baby all right?"

"Too much milk after dinner, I'm afraid."

Alex lowered his hand. "Another accident?"

"All over poor Bailey."

Mateo was no stranger to babies' assortment of surprises. He not only cared for pregnant women before and during delivery, he looked after their concerns postpartum. Many days, his practice was filled with the sights, sounds and smells of children of all ages. He'd been chucked up on more often than some people brushed their teeth. Part of the job. He wasn't sure Bailey would be quite so cool with it, particularly given the trying day she'd had.

Setting down his glass, Mateo rose too. "I'll take her home."

"No need. Bailey's fine," Natalie said. "Other than needing a quick shower and a fresh change of clothes, and I have a stack of outfits in my pre-baby wardrobe she can wear." She ran her hand down her husband's sleeve. "Tammy's settling the baby now. I'll go see how Bailey's doing."

As she sailed away, Alex fell back into his chair. The grin on his face said it all. "She's an amazing woman, isn't she?"

"You're a lucky man."

Alex leaned closer and lowered his voice. "So, now we know they'll be occupied for a while yet, tell me about it."

"Tell you what?"

"About your date."

"She's not a *date*."

"She's an attractive female accompanying you to dinner. If she's not a date, what is she?"

"Difficult to work out," Mateo admitted. "Like I said on the phone, she appeared on my doorstep yesterday morning." He went into more about the engagement and her dramatic flight from Italy, the loan and Bailey's search for a job to pay it back. "When I phoned Mama today, she confirmed that she'd told Bailey to drop in." Mateo dropped his gaze to the glass he rotated between his fingers. "Mama also asked me to watch out for her until she can make amends with her father."

"Trouble there too?"

"I'm sure whatever's gone on before could be sorted out with one or two calm conversations."

"Family rifts aren't usually that easy to solve." Alex took a long sip of scotch.

"Either way, it's none of my business."

"So where's Bailey staying?"

"I said she could stay with me—just for a few days." Alex coughed as if his drink had gone down the wrong way. Mateo frowned. "What?"

Alex tried to contain his amused look. "Nothing. I mean, Bailey seems very nice."

"But?"

"But nothing, Mateo. I'm only surprised that you've opened your home to her. You haven't done that in a while."

"You mean since Linda." Mateo slid his glass onto the side table. "This isn't the same."

Alex studied his friend's face and, inhaling, nodded and changed the subject.

"What's happening with the vacation?"

"I haven't made any firm decisions yet."

"But you're still going to France, right?"

It was more a statement than a question. His annual pilgrimage to Ville Laube was a duty he never shirked. But, of course, it was more than simply an obligation. He enjoyed catching up with the people who ran the orphanage. Although seeing the children conjured up as many haunted feelings as good. Each year he saw so many new faces as well as those who had lived there for years.

One little boy was a favorite. Remy had turned five last visit. Dark hair and eyes, solemn until you pitched him a ball—any kind. Then his face would light up. He reminded Mateo of himself at that age. Leaving Remy last year had been difficult.

When he returned this year, Mateo hoped that little boy was gone. He hoped he'd found a good family who would love and support him. He wondered what kind of man Remy would grow into. If he would learn from the right influences. Whether he'd always have plenty to eat.

Mateo confirmed, "I'll go to France."

"Maybe Bailey would like to go too."

Mateo all but lost his breath. Then he swore. "You're not trying to step into Mama Celeca's matchmaking shoes, I hope."

"Just an idea. You seem...interested."

"You saw us together for less than a minute."

"It was all the time I needed to see that you think she's different."

"Hold on." Mateo got to his feet. "Just because you've found the one, doesn't mean I need to be pushed down any aisle."

"Maybe it'd make a difference if you didn't fight it quite so hard?"

"Fight what?"

Both men's attention flew in the direction of that third voice. Natalie stood in the living room doorway. While Mateo withered—*was Bailey a step behind, within earshot?*—Alex pushed to his feet and crossed to his wife.

"Nothing, honey," he said, stealing a quick kiss. "Is the baby okay? How's Bailey?"

"Judge for yourselves."

When a stylish woman, wearing an exquisite pink cocktail number and glittering diamond drop earrings, slid into the room, Mateo did a double take then all but fell back into his seat.

Bailey?

While the bikini-girl turned glamour-queen crossed the room, looking as if she'd worn Chanel all her life, Natalie clasped her hands under her chin and exclaimed, "Isn't she gorgeous?"

Mateo knew he was smiling. He wanted to agree. Unfortunately he was too stunned—too delighted—to find his voice.

"The first time Mateo and I came to this place, we were twenty-two," Alex explained as a uniformed Maxim's waiter showed the foursome to a table next to the dance floor.

"Twenty-three," Mateo amended, his hand a touch away from Bailey's elbow as they navigated tables of patrons enjoying their meals and tasteful atmosphere, including tinkling background music. "You'd just had a cast off your arm after a spill on your skateboard."

"You rode a skateboard at twenty-three?" Natalie laughed as she lowered into a chair the waiter had pulled out for her.

Alex ran a finger and thumb down his tie. "And very well, might I add."

While the waiter draped linen napkins over laps, Bailey tried to contain the nerves jitterbugging in her belly. She'd dined at similar establishments, although not since her mother had died. In the old days her family had enjoyed dinner out at least once a week, but never to this particular restaurant. Wearing this glamorous dress and these dazzling earrings, not to mention the fabulous silver heels, she felt as if a magic wand had been waved and she'd emerged from her baby throw-up moment as a returned modern-day princess. For a day that had started out horrendously, she was feeling pretty fine now. Not even tired. Although catch-up jet lag would probably hit when she least expected it.

Until then she'd lap up what promised to be a wonderful night.

Some people you couldn't help but like. Natalie and Alex were that kind of folk. And Mateo…she'd wondered what he'd be like in friends' company. His smile was broader. His laugh, deeper. And when his gaze caught hers, the interested approval in his heavy-lidded eyes left her feeling surreal and believing that tonight they might have met for the first time.

"I must confess," Natalie said, casting an eye over the menu. "I love not having to think about the dishes."

"I help with that," Alex pointed out, teasing.

"And I love you for it." Natalie snatched a kiss from her husband's cheek then found Bailey's gaze. "Do you like to cook?"

"I'm no expert. But I would like to learn how to prepare meals the way they do in Italy." The dishes she'd enjoyed there had been so incredibly tasty and wholesome.

Natalie tipped her head toward Mateo. "You know your date's a bit of a chef?"

Her *date?*

Hoping no one noticed her blush, Bailey merely replied, "Really?"

"We go over for dinner at least every month," Natalie added.

Mateo qualified, "Nothing fancy. Just a way of remembering home."

"His crepes are mouth-watering," Natalie confided.

Bailey thought for a moment. "Aren't crepes French?"

"Mateo spent his first years there." As soon as the words were out, Natalie's expression dropped. "That probably wasn't my place to say."

While Mateo waved it off, Bailey puzzled over what the drama with France could be. He must have seen her curiosity.

"I lived in an orphanage the first six years of my life."

All the air left Bailey's lungs as images of dank, dark corridors and rickety cots with children who lacked love's warm touch swam up in her mind. She couldn't imagine it, particularly not for Mateo Celeca. Her lips moved a few times before she got out a single, "Oh."

"It wasn't so bad," Mateo said, obviously reading her expression. "The people who ran it were kind. We had what we needed."

"Mateo sponsors the orphanage now," Alex chipped in as, wine menu in hand, he beckoned a waiter.

Bailey sat back. Of course. Yesterday Mateo had mentioned he was a benefactor. She hadn't thought beyond the notion that any donations would be the act of someone who had the means to make a difference to others' lives. She hadn't stopped to think his work in France might be more personal. That he was paying homage to a darker past and wanted to help those who were in the same underprivileged position he'd once been.

"It's difficult for them to find funds," Mateo was saying, pouring more water. "A small bit goes a long way."

"You're too modest," Alex said.

Natalie added, "Wouldn't surprise me if one day you come back with someone who needs a good home."

"I'm hardly in a position."

Mateo's reply sounded unaffected. But Bailey detected a certain faraway gleam in his eye. Would Mateo consider adopting if he *were* in the position? If he were married?

She tried to focus on Natalie's words...something about looking forward to dessert. But, as much as she tried, Bailey couldn't shake the vision of Mateo playing with a child of his own with a faceless Mrs. Celeca smiling and gazing on. Not her, of course. She wasn't after a husband—or certainly not this soon after her recent hairy experience. One day she wanted to be part of a loving couple—like Natalie and Alex— but right now she was more than happy to be free.

Did Mateo feel the same way? Natalie wondered, stealing a glance at the doctor from beneath her lashes. Or could Mama's perennial bachelor be on the lookout for a suitable wife slash mother for an adopted child?

* * *

Finishing dessert, a moist, scrumptious red velvet cake, Bailey gave a soft cry when some chocolate sauce slipped from her spoon and caught the bodice of her dress. She slid a fingertip over the spot to scoop up the drop, which only smeared the sauce. Bailey didn't wear these kinds of labels, but she knew something about the price tags. Often they cost more than her airfare home.

With dread filling her stomach, Bailey turned to Natalie. "I'll pay to have it dry-cleaned."

But Natalie wasn't troubled.

"Keep the dress, if you want. It's too snug on me after the baby anyway. In fact, there's a heap of things you could take off my hands, if you'd like."

Eyes down, Bailey dabbed the spot with her napkin. She was grateful for the offer but also embarrassed. Over dinner, they'd discussed her travels and lightly touched on the Emilio affair. Mention had been made of Mateo's suggestion she stay a couple of days as well as Natalie's proposal of work. Now the offer of a designer wardrobe...

She was beginning to feel as if she constantly had her hand out.

Bailey set aside the napkin. "That's very kind, Natalie. But you don't need to do that."

"Chances are I won't wear them again. Some mothers are eager to get back their pre-baby bodies but I quite like the fuller me."

"Hear, hear," her husband cooed close to her ear. "Now if you've finished dessert, what say we dance? Just you and me."

Natalie laughed. "Oh, you love when the three of us dance together in the living room."

"Of course." Alex kissed her hand and found his feet. "But this moment I'm happy to have only you in my arms."

As they headed for the dance floor, Bailey sighed.

"You're right. They're a magic couple. Have they been together long? The way they look at each other, anyone would guess they'd fallen in love yesterday."

"They've been together a couple of years."

"I thought they might have been school sweethearts," she said, watching them slow dance to the soft strains of a love song drifting through the room while misty beams played over their heads.

"Natalie grew up in far different circumstances than she enjoys now. Very humble beginnings."

Bailey was taken aback. "She looks as if she might've been born into royalty."

"Tonight, so do you."

Bailey's breath caught high in her chest. Was he merely being polite or was the compliment meant to have the reaction it did? Suddenly she didn't know where to look. What to say. But her mother had said to always take a compliment graciously. So, gathering herself, she lifted her eyes to his and smiled. "Thank you."

Her heart was thumping too loudly to maintain that eye contact, however, so she found Alex and Natalie on the dance floor. Natalie was laughing at something her husband had said while Alex gazed down at his wife adoringly. They radiated wedded bliss.

"It was a good day," Mateo said.

"Which day?"

"The day I helped bring their son into the world."

Elbow on the table, Bailey rested her chin in the cup of her hand. "I bet you had everything prepared and everyone on their toes."

"Quite the opposite. When she went into labor, we were at Alex's beachside holiday house. It happened quickly." He peered over toward the couple. Natalie's cheek was resting on Alex's shoulder now. "She'd miscarried years before. Alex was concerned for mother and child both."

"But nothing went wrong?"

Mateo smiled across. "You saw Reece tonight."

Bailey relaxed. "Perfect."

"Alex had always longed for a son."

"I suppose most men do," she said, wondering if she'd get a reaction.

"Most men...yes." Then, as if to put an end to that conversation, he stood and held out his hand. "Would you care to dance?"

Bailey's throat closed. Perhaps she should have seen that coming but she was at a loss for words. Mateo looked so tall and heart-stoppingly handsome, gazing down at her with those dark, penetrating eyes. Eyes that constantly intrigued her. She wanted to accept his offer. Wanted the opportunity to know the answer to her earlier question—how it would feel to have his arms surround her. Here, in this largely neutral, populated setting, she could find out.

She placed her hand in his. That telling warmth rose again, tingling over her flesh, heating her cheeks and her neck. His eyes seemed to smile into hers as she found her feet and together they moved to the dance floor, occupied by other couples, some absorbed more in the song than their partner, others locked in each other's arms and ardent gazes.

Bailey couldn't stop her heart from hammering as Mateo turned and rested a hot palm low on her back while bringing their still-clasped hands to his lapel. Concentrating to level her breathing, she slid and rested her left hand over the broad slope of his shoulder at the same time the tune segued into an even slower, more romantic song and the lights dimmed a fraction more.

They began to move and instantly Bailey was gripped by the heat radiating from his body, burrowing into and warming hers. Her senses seemed heightened. She was infinitely aware of his thumb circling over the dip in her back. Her lungs celebrated being filled with his mesmerizing scent. Strangely, all the happenings around them faded into a suddenly bland background. When a corner of his mouth slanted—the corner with that small scar—her pulse rate spiked and her blood began to sizzle. She'd wanted to know. Now she did. Having Mateo's arms around her—soothing and at the same time exciting her—was like being held by some kind of god.

"So you'll be working for Natalie's agency?"

"While I was dressing—make that *re*dressing—Natalie explained they'd lost three cleaners in the past couple of weeks."

"You don't mind the work?"

"I'm grateful for it. And it won't be forever."

He grinned. "Sounds as if you're making plans."

Seeing her father today cemented what she'd already come to realize. Education was the key to independence. "I'm going to apply to college."

"Do you know what you'll study? Teaching? Nursing?"

"Maybe I should become a doctor," she joked. "Dr. Bailey Ross. Neurosurgeon." She laughed and so did he, but not in a condescending way. "I want to do something that makes people happy," she went on. "That makes them feel good about themselves."

"Whatever you choose I'm sure you'll do well."

"Because you know I'm an A student, right?"

"Because I think you have guts. Persistence will get you most places in life."

Unless you were talking about her father. The more she'd tried, the more he'd turned his back. Cut her off. There came a time when a person needed to accept they should look forward rather than back.

But then she retraced her thoughts back to Mateo's

words—*I think you have guts*. She gave him a dubious look. "Was that another compliment?"

A line cut between his brows. "Tell you what. We'll make a deal. I promise not to mention the money you owe Mama in a derogatory way if you promise something in return. It has to do with my vacation."

She couldn't think what. Except maybe, "You want me to house sit?"

"I want you to come with me to France."

Bailey's legs buckled. When she fell against him, bands of steel stopped her from slipping farther. But the way her front grazed against his, his help only made her sudden case of weakness worse.

Siphoning down a breath, she scooped back some hair fallen over her face. "Sorry. Did you just say you want me to go to France with you?"

"I got the impression you hadn't seen Paris."

"I was saving it for last. I never got there."

His smile flashed white beneath the purple lights. "Now's your chance."

She took a step back but more deep breaths didn't help. She cupped her forehead.

"Mateo, I'm confused."

He brought her near again and flicked a glance over his shoulder at the couple dancing nearby. "Blame Alex. He suggested it."

She tried to ignore the delicious press of his body, the masculine scent of his skin, the way his hard thigh nudged between hers as he rotated them around in a tight circle. "You know I don't have money for a ticket to Europe." Her jaw hardened. "And I won't take any more charity."

"Even if you'd be doing me a favor, keeping me company?" His dark gaze, so close, roamed her face. "One good turn deserves another."

"That's not fair."

His mouth turned into a solemn line. "There wouldn't be any conditions."

Bailey blinked. Maybe because he was Mama's grandson, she hadn't considered he might be trying to buy more than her company.

With the lights slowly spinning and couples floating by, oxygen burned in her lungs while she tried to come up with an appropriate reply to a question that had knocked her for a loop. After an agonizingly long moment, she felt the groan rumble in his chest and his grip on her hand loosen.

"You're right," he said. "Crazy idea."

"It's not that I wouldn't *like* to go." She'd always wanted to see Paris. It was her biggest disappointment that she'd planned to save France for last rather than enjoying that country first. "But I've just got back," she explained. "I'm starting that job Monday." She finished with the obvious excuse. "We don't know each other."

He dismissed it with a self-deprecating smile. "Like I said. Forget I spoke."

But as his palm skimmed up her back and he tucked her crown under his chin while they continued to dance, although she knew she really should, Bailey couldn't forget.

At the end of the evening, she and Mateo dropped Natalie and Alex off then drove back to his place in a loaded silence.

Her breathing was heavier than it ought to be. Was his heartbeat hammering as fast as hers, or was she the only one who couldn't get that enthralling dance and tempting offer out of her mind? Mateo had asked her to jet away to France with him. What had he been thinking? What was she thinking still considering it after having already told him no?

Bailey pressed on her stomach as her insides looped.

Admittedly, she was uniquely attracted to Mateo Celeca; he had a presence, a confidence that was difficult to ignore. But how did she feel about him beyond the physical? Yesterday, after he'd tried to degrade her over the money she'd loaned, she'd thought him little more than a self-serving snob. And yet, tonight, when she'd met his friends...had been his *date*...

Her stomach looped again.

After that episode with Emilio, the last thing she wanted was to get caught up in a man. Any man. Even when he gave generously to the orphanage where he'd spent his earliest years. Even when she felt as if she'd found a slice of heaven in his arms.

Since that dance, the air between them had crackled with a double dose of anticipation and electricity. If, when they got home, they started talking, got to touching, she didn't know if she'd want to stop.

After they pulled into the garage, Mateo opened her door and helped her out. Their hands lingered, the contact simmered, before his fingers slipped from hers and he moved to unlock the internal door and flick on the lights. Gathering herself—straightening her dress and patting down her burning cheeks—Bailey followed into the kitchen.

"Care for a nightcap?" he asked, poised near the fridge.

Bailey clasped the pocketbook Natalie had loaned her under her chin and, resolute, made a believable excuse.

"I'm beat. Practically dead on my feet. Think I'll go straight up and turn in."

As she headed out, Bailey laughed at herself. He might not even *want* to kiss her. She could be blowing this awareness factor all out of proportion. But prevention was always better than cure. She'd accepted his invitation to stay a couple more nights. She didn't want to do something they both might regret in the morning. And if they got involved that way, there *would* be regrets. Neither was looking for a relationship. She certainly didn't want to get caught up in a man who, only yesterday, had as good as called her thief. A man who might set her pulse racing but who could never get serious about a woman in her situation.

And yet, he had asked her to France....

When Mateo reached the foot of the staircase, he stopped and turned to face her. Standing there, simply gazing at one another in the semi-darkness, she had this silly urge to play down the scene, stick out a hand and offer to shake. But, given past experience, probably best they didn't touch.

"Thank you for the lovely evening," she said.

"You're welcome."

Still, he didn't move.

"Well…" Clutching her pocketbook tighter, she set a foot onto the lowest stair. "Good night."

"Good night, Bailey."

When she began to climb, he started up too. They ascended together until they hit a point where the stairs divided into separate branches. A fork in the road.

Her stomach twisting with nerves, she chanced a look across. He was looking at her too, a masculine silhouette a mere arm's length away.

Swirling desire pooled low in her belly and she frowned. "You're not moving."

"Neither are you."

Rolling back her shoulders, she issued a firm and final, "Good night."

She hiked the rest of the stairs, right to the top. But before she could head off down to her suite, curiosity won out again. She edged a gaze over her right shoulder, to where she'd left Mateo standing seconds ago. What she saw sent her heart dropping in her chest.

He was gone. And wasn't that what she'd wanted? What she knew was best for both their sakes?

Still, she stared at that vacant spot a moment more, feeling strangely empty and no longer so pretty in her pink designer dress. Shifting her weight, she finally rotated back...and ran right into Mateo's solid chest.

Her heels balanced on the edge of the stairs, Bailey toppled back. But before she could fall, his arm hooked around her waist, pulling her effortlessly against him. *Déjà vu*. With the bodice of her dress pinned to his chest—with every one of her reflexes in a tailspin—she worked to catch her breath before croaking out, "I thought you were tired."

"*You* said you were tired." His dark eyes gleamed. "I'm wide awake."

When she felt his hardness pressed against her belly, she gulped down another breath only to feel him grow harder still. Any doubts she may have had were blown away. The way her own blood was throbbing, taking this steadily growing attraction further seemed frighteningly inevitable.

"Maybe..." She wet her suddenly dry lips. "Maybe we should have that nightcap after all."

His gaze dropped to her lips. "What kind of nightcap?"

"What would you like?"

His mouth came to within a whisper of hers.

"I'd like you."

Six

He didn't waste time waiting for her reply. Bailey supposed he saw all he needed to know in her eyes. He angled and, before she could think beyond *I need you to kiss me,* she was in his arms and he was moving down the hall, away from her suite, headed for his.

The tall double doors of his suite were open. He didn't bother to kick them shut after he'd carried her through. Nor did he switch on any lamps. What she could make out in the shadows was courtesy of the light filtering in from the hall as well as the moonbeams slanting through a bank of soaring arched windows that looked out over that garden and its statues below.

He stopped at the foot of his bed and his voice dropped to a low rasp.

"This is what you want?"

Instinctively, her palm wove around the sandpaper of his

jaw. She filled her lungs with his scent then skimmed the pad of her thumb over the dent in his chin.

"Yes," she murmured.

His chest expanded, his grip tightened then he lifted her higher in his arms as his head came purposefully down. When his mouth claimed hers, Bailey couldn't contain the moan of deepest desire the sensation dragged from her throat. She didn't want to contain *anything*. And as his mouth worked magic against hers and his stubble grazed and teased her skin, she pressed herself up and in, needing to feel even closer. Needing him as close as it got.

Her fingers wound through his hair while his throat rumbled with satisfaction and the kiss deepened. Even as her mind and body raged with desire, she was lucid enough to recognize the simple truth. Whatever it was that had sparked when they'd met, it had grown to a point where now they were downright hungry for each other. *Starving* for each other's touch in a primal nothing-held-back, nothing-taboo, kind of way. She could never get enough of this burn...of the flames that already leapt and blazed nearly out of control.

When his lips gradually left hers, she felt dizzy. Her eyes remained closed but she heard and felt his breathing. At the edges of her mind, she wondered...why was this coming together so intense? So combustible?

He dipped to sit her on the edge of the mattress. With moonlight spilling in, she dragged the dress up over her head then, in her lingerie, watched as he wound the shirt off his shoulders, the sleeves from his arms. When he was naked, he bent near, slid an arm around her waist and drew her up to stand again. Holding her chin, he ran the wet tip of his tongue along the open seam of her mouth while, at her back, he unsnapped the strapless bra with one deft flick. His palm pressed down the dent of her spine and slipped into the back of her panties. She whimpered as her womb contracted and quivered…a tantalizing prelude to the climax she couldn't wait to enjoy.

His fingertips pressed and seared into her flesh while his mouth covered hers completely again, and all the time her insides clenched and pulsed while her limbs and mind went to mush. She wanted this heaven to go on forever. But even more, she wanted him bearing down on top of her. Inside of her. Filling and fulfilling her *now*.

Her hands ironed down his sides. When she reached his lean hips, she urged him forward, toward her and the bed. With their mouths still joined, she felt his smile before he broke the kiss long enough to wrench back the sheets. With a determined gleam in his eyes, he crowded until the back of her legs met the cool edge of the mattress. His big hands ringed her waist and her feet left the ground long enough for him to lay her gently down. He followed a heartbeat behind.

Looming above her, everything seemed to still as he searched her eyes in a world of midnight shadows. His deep low voice seemed to fill the room.

"I didn't ask you to stay here for this."

She drew an aimless pattern through the hair at the base of his throat.

"I know."

"Although I'm not sorry you agreed."

She matched his grin. "I'm not sorry you asked."

He dropped a tender kiss at the side of her mouth, a barely there touch that shot a fountain of star-tipped sparks through her every fiber.

"Come with me to France," he murmured against her lips.

She groaned. The temptation was huge. She'd said no and had meant it. She was starting a job Monday. She didn't want to take more charity. But those considerations didn't seem quite so solid since he'd carried her to his bed.

Closing her eyes, she sighed. He was kissing the sensitive spot beneath her left lobe.

"What if I say please?"

She bit her lip. He was *killing* her.

"I'll tell you what." She filed her fingers up over his burning ears, through his hair. "I promise not to say no again if you promise not to ask."

He moved lower to nuzzle the arc of her neck. "I don't like when you say no."

"To everything but that, Mateo..." She hooked her leg around his hip and drew him close. *"Yes, yes, yes."*

Mateo couldn't stop to think about how his unexpected encounter with Bailey Ross had come to this. How they'd gone from strangers to opponents to lovers in less than two days. As he tasted a leisurely line along the perfumed sweep of her shoulder, he only knew these sensations were too intense to analyze. More intense—more vital—than he'd ever had before.

When her heel dug into the back of his thigh, letting him know again she was on the same page, he ground up against her but then grit his teeth and blocked that insistent heady push. Tonight would be sweet torture. He'd need every ounce of willpower to keep this encounter—his pleasure—from peaking too soon.

Working to steady his breathing, his pace, he sculpted a palm over the outside of one full breast as he shifted lower. His mouth covered that nipple before his teeth grazed up all the way, tugging the tip of the bead. Her hands had been winding through his hair but now she dug in and held on as she shuddered and moaned beneath him. He heard her desperate swallow and listened, pleased that her breathing sounded more labored than his own. Savoring the way her breasts rose and fell on each lungful of air, he twirled his tongue around that tip and tried to ignore the fact his every inch was ready to explode.

With her leg twined over the back of his, her pelvis began to move in time with the adoring sweep of his tongue. She murmured something he didn't catch. But he wouldn't ask and stop the bone-melting rhythm their bodies had fallen into. He didn't want to interrupt for a moment the feel of her body stirring beneath his. He could lie here all night, doing precisely this.

If only his erection wasn't begging for more.

He repositioned again, higher to savor the honey of her lips at the same time his touch wove down: over her ribs, the curve of her waist, the subtle flare of a hip, then up over the same terrain. He was performing a repeat descent, stroking and playing—anticipating the added treasures he'd discover this time around—when she grunted, shifted and pushed against his chest.

He froze. Then, eyes snapping open, he rolled away. What was wrong? Had he hurt her?

When she slid over too—on *top* of him—he held his brow and almost laughed with relief.

"What are you doing?"

Crouched on his lap, she slid her hips one way and the other then tossed back the hair fallen over her face. "What do you think?"

She slid *up* a little this time then down over his throbbing shaft. That sent him reeling way too close to the edge. He was thrilled she was so completely in the zone that she wanted to take the reins, but any more of that kind of maneuvering and he'd reach the finish line way too soon.

He flipped her over so she lay on her back again, him firmly on top. While she peered up at him, a saucy glint in her eyes, his hand burrowed between them, down the front of her panties, and his erection grew heavier still. She was warm and moist. When his touch curled up between her folds and pressed against a woman's most sensitive spot, she let out a time honored sound that told him she was ready.

Leaning over, he opened his bedside drawer, found the pack then tore a single foiled wrap with his teeth. As he rolled on protection, her fingers sluiced up and down his sides. Oh, he wanted to take this slower. Make it last. But this time, with this lady, that wasn't going to happen.

Sheathed, he positioned himself, took a long slow kiss from her welcoming mouth then eased inside. Her walls clamped around him at the same time her hips lifted and she opened her mouth wider, inviting him deeper.

With one arm curled around her head, he drove in and clenched every muscle as a mind-tingling burn hardened him more. He felt as if he was drowning in a lake of fire. All exposed nerve endings and profound sizzling need.

Bailey trailed her fingers down his neck, felt the cords bulging and pulsing, and melted more. The way he moved with her left her breathless while his mouth on hers raised her up. She wanted this moment to go on forever. Never wanted the steep waves of pleasure to wane or fade. And yet they both needed to go that bit further. Needed to be thrown up to the stars and explode on their way back down.

He was snatching slow kisses from her brow, from her cheek, holding her hip securely as his strokes grew ever stronger and longer. The friction was scolding, the pleasure beyond what she could take.

And then his kisses stopped and his body grew still and hard. She sensed his every tendon stretched trip wire tight, could feel his heart thumping and pounding in his ears. The mind-altering fire at her core intensified, somehow changing in dimension and in shape. Then, in one finite moment, in less time than it took to suck down a breath, all the universe contracted into a single high-voltage speck. Beyond that nothing existed. Nothing but black.

When he thrust again—when he hit that secret wanting spot—she threw back her head, spread her wings and flew.

Seven

"Tell me more about France."

At the sound of Bailey's voice filtering though the predawn mist, Mateo lifted his head off the pillow and dropped a kiss on her silky crown.

They'd made love well into the night. The first time had been incredible. Incomparable. But over far too quickly. The second time they'd slowed down enough to thoroughly explore each other's bodies and share their most intimate needs. The third time they'd come apart in each other's arms might have been the best…the time when he'd truly begun to see that this joining meant more than simply great sex. The connection they shared, the amazing way they fit, was special.

That didn't mean he'd changed his mind about getting serious. About settling down. Invariably marriage meant children. Children of his own. But his practice was his life. He'd put all he had into doing his best and building a home that was his. He had everything he needed. Everything and more. He felt secure, and that was life's most valuable gift.

If he were to become a husband...a father...well, he couldn't think of a more vulnerable place to be. There were concerns over the complications in the womb, worry about childhood disease, not to mention the fact that in this world he had no living family now, other than Mama. If fate stepped in and left his child without parents...

Mateo swallowed against the pit formed in his throat.

This is why he never let himself analyze relationships too deeply, particularly following the "after all she could get" Linda incident. He was a man of influence and means who could choose what course his life should take. Tonight he'd chosen to act on the undeniable chemistry he shared with Bailey. Given she'd asked about France a moment ago, he hoped they could continue to enjoy the attraction a while longer. For however long it might last.

Nestled in the crook of his arm, she twined to rest her chin on her thatched hands, which lay on one side of his chest.

"What's it like?" She asked, looking beautifully rumpled and sleep deprived but content. "Everyone seems to love Paris. Did you ever get into the city when you were young?"

"As a child?"

"Uh-huh."

"I didn't know Paris existed."

She sat up a little, bracing her weight on an elbow as she searched his eyes in the misty light. Outside, the morning sun peeked over the distant rise, painting a translucent halo around her head.

Her voice softened when she asked, "Were you very lonely there? At the orphanage, I mean."

Mateo's jaw tensed. His first instinct was to push her question aside. If anyone, including Alex or Natalie, brought up his childhood, he rarely gave away too much. The past was past...even if it was never forgotten.

But lying here with Bailey after the extraordinary night they'd shared, he felt closer to her this minute than anyone he'd known. That shouldn't be. He'd loved and respected Ernesto. He adored Mama. He had friends he would do anything for and, he was certain, vice versa.

And yet, he couldn't deny it. Whatever drew him to Bailey Ross was a force unto itself. He wanted to share more than his bed with her tonight. He wanted to open up...at least this once.

"I wasn't lonely," he began. "I had many friends and adults I knew that cared for us all." He thought more deeply and frowned. "I did feel *alone,* which is different, but I was too young to understand why. I never knew my parents. No one explained about the 'who' or the 'when.' I didn't realize a life outside the orphanage existed until my fifth birthday."

Sitting up, she wrapped the sheet around her breasts, under her arms. "What happened on your birthday? I don't suppose you had a party."

"From what I can recall, the day was pleasant enough. Everyone sang to me after lunch. I got a special dessert along with two friends I picked out." He searched his memory and blinked then smiled. "I received a gift. People from town donated them. I tore open the paper and found a wooden train. Green chimney," he recalled. "Red wheels. I thought I was made." But his smile slipped. "Then my best friend said he was going away. That a mother and father were taking him home."

Bailey tucked her knees up and hugged her sheet-clad legs. "It mustn't have made sense."

He flinched at a familiar pang in his chest and for a moment he wanted to end that conversation and talk about the France people found in travel books. The "gay Paree" with which Bailey would identify. But she wasn't listening to this story to snatch some voyeuristic thrill. He saw from her unguarded expression that she wanted to learn more about the man she'd made love with tonight. He wanted to learn more about her too. So, to be fair, he took a breath and went on.

"I knew some children were there with us, then, suddenly, they weren't. No one spoke about it, or if they did, I didn't have the maturity to latch on and work the steps out. But this time, with Henri, I began to see."

"You realized something was missing."

He nodded.

Yes, missing. Exactly.

"From a second-story window," he said, "where the boys slept, I watched Henri slide into a shiny white car and drive away with two people, a man and woman. I shouted out and waved, but he didn't look up. Not until the last minute. Then he saw me. I think he called out my name, too."

With her blue eyes glittering in the early dawn light, she tipped nearer and held his arm.

"Oh, Mateo…that must have been awful."

Not *awful.* "Eye-opening. Unsettling. From then on I was more aware of others leaving. More aware that I was left behind. I tried to find him a few years back. It would be great to see him again. Hear if his memories match mine."

Henri had been his first friend.

Mateo touched the scar on his upper lip—the one he'd received when Henri had thrown a ball too hard and he'd missed catching it—then, dismissing the pang in his chest, he swung his legs over the side of the bed and reached for the water decanter. After pouring two glasses, he offered her one.

She drank, watching him over the rim of her glass.

"How did Mama Celeca find you?" she asked, handing the empty glass back.

"Not Mama. Ernesto." He took another mouthful and set both glasses down. "Years before, he'd been in love with a woman who'd carried his child. A friend, returning from France, let Ernesto know he'd heard that Antoinette had given birth in a town called Ville Laube and had offered her baby boy up for adoption there. Ernesto flew straight over. He found the orphanage his friend had described but not his boy."

Clutching the sheet under her chin, Bailey sagged.

"I thought you'd say that *you* were Ernesto's child."

"Not through blood. But apparently my parents were Italian, too. I was left there when I was three, but I don't remember any life before the orphanage."

She shifted and he waited until she'd settled alongside of him.

"One day after Henri had gone," he went on, "I saw this sad looking man sitting alone in the courtyard under a huge oak. His hands were clasped between his thighs. His eyes were downcast. When I edged closer, I saw they were bloodshot. He'd been crying. I knew because some times in the mornings I had bloodshot eyes too."

His throat closed as the memory grew stronger and flooded his mind with a mix of emotions, sounds and smells from the past. The scent of lavender. The noise of children playing. The deepest feeling that, if only he knew this sad man, he would like him.

But, "I didn't know why the man was unhappy. I had no idea what to say. I only knew I felt for him. So I sat down and put my hand over his."

Mateo looked across. In the growing light, he thought he saw a single tear speed down Bailey's cheek. Ironic, because after that day he couldn't remember ever crying again.

"And he took you home," she said.

"Home to Italy, yes. And later here to Australia."

"So Mama Celeca isn't your real grandmother?"

"She's always treated me as though she is. She accepted me from the moment Ernesto brought me back to Casa Buona. I helped Ernesto in his office during the day and hung out with Mama in the kitchen in the evenings."

"Where she taught you to cook."

Remembering the aromas and Mama's careful instructions, he smiled and nodded. "The old-fashioned way."

"The *best* way." She turned more toward him. "Did Ernesto find his boy?"

"No." And that was the tragedy. "Although he never gave up hope."

"Did he ever marry?"

"Never. He died two years ago."

"I remember. Mama told me."

"He wanted to be buried back home. Mama was heartbroken at her son's death, but that, at least, gave her a measure of comfort." He voiced the words that were never far from his heart. "He was a good son. A good father. Last year I had a call from a woman, Ernesto's biological son's widow. After he'd been killed in a hit-and-run, she'd found papers from the orphanage that helped her track Ernesto down. She'd wanted him to know."

She lowered her head and murmured, so softly, he barely heard. "Is all this why Natalie thinks you might bring home a child from France one day?"

"Adoption rules were more flexible in the country back then."

"You'd have no trouble proving you could care for a child. I haven't known you long but I know you'd make a good father…like Ernesto."

A knot twisted in his chest. Sharp. Uncomfortable. He'd already explained.

"I'm too busy for a child." He looked inside and, flinching, admitted, "Too selfish."

When his temple throbbed, he turned to plump up his pillow. They ought to get some sleep, Bailey especially.

They lay down again, front to front, curled up tight. Mateo was drifting when she murmured against his chest.

"When are you expected in France?"

"Next week."

"I told Natalie I'd start work for her in two days' time." She lifted her head to glance out the window at the ever-rising sun. "Make that tomorrow."

Mateo was suddenly wide awake. If Bailey was thinking about changing her mind and coming with him…

"Natalie won't hold anything against you for taking a week off."

In fact, he was sure she'd be happy at the news. Natalie made no secret of the fact that she would love to see her husband's best friend settled with someone nice. Not that that was in the cards.

She snuggled into him more. "I'd feel as if I were copping out."

"Visiting the Eiffel Tower, the Louvre, perhaps. But the orphanage?" He skimmed a hand down her smooth warm arm. "It's not a cop-out."

After several minutes, her breathing grew deeper and he thought she was finally asleep. He was letting oblivion overtake him too when she spoke again.

"Mama's right."

He forced his heavy lids open. "About what?"

She rubbed her cheek against his chest and murmured in a groggy voice, "You are a good man."

Eight

As Mateo predicted, Natalie wasn't the least bit upset when the following day, Bailey rang to explain.

"I know I'm only starting," she began, sitting behind Mateo's desk in his home office. "I'm so grateful for the chance, but I was wondering if I could possibly ask for the week after next off?"

"Are you all right?"

"I feel great." In fact, better than great. "Mateo asked whether I might like to fly with him to France."

Bailey jerked the receiver from her ear as Natalie squealed down the line.

"Sorry," Natalie said. "I'm just excited for you. For you both. And I'll need to go through my wardrobe with a fine-tooth comb. In late October, you're going to need some warm clothes over there."

The following day Bailey dived into the first of her cleaning jobs. The work was constant and anything but glamorous, but she rolled up her sleeves and took pride in making sure the floors were spotless and that the kitchens and bathrooms sparkled. She was being constructive, pushing forward, earning her way and feeling rewarded because of it.

When Friday came, Bailey was exhausted by the time she got to Mateo's place. But she was also elated. When he opened the door for her, she threw out her hand.

Mateo took the slip of paper she held. "What's this?"

"A printout of the receipt from my transfer."

Mateo had set up an account solely for the purpose of her loan repayments.

When he smiled, he truly looked pleased.

"We should celebrate."

"What do you suggest?"

"Dinner at this little Italian taverna five minutes from here. Unless you're too tired…"

"No." Suddenly she was feeling pepped up. She *should* celebrate. This was a noteworthy step toward reaching her goals. "But on one condition. I pay my way."

One brow hiked up. "You're supposed to be saving, not spending."

"We go dutch or we don't go."

They went and enjoyed a carafe of Chianti, twirled and slurped spaghetti, paid half each and, when they arrived home, made love as they'd done every night since their first.

Afterward, as they lay tangled in each other's arms and Mateo stroked her hair, Bailey thought back on the week, feeling happier than she had in a long while. She'd had fun backpacking around Europe and she'd enjoyed herself in Italy—before Emilio had cornered her the way he had. But now, here with Mateo, she'd stepped up to a different level of understanding.

Funnily enough, she felt settled. Living in this grand palace with a strong-minded millionaire doctor…unbelievable, but she felt as if she belonged.

But this hyper exhilaration was only temporary. It wasn't real. Wouldn't last. Staying in this extraordinary house with this extraordinary man was a fairy tale she happened to fall into. Clearly, Mateo had been with other women but he'd never committed, as Mama had told her more than once. There was no reason to believe that what they'd shared this week would last either.

She was a big girl. She was fine with that.

Smoothing a palm over his chest, she smiled softly. This time with Mateo might be temporary, but she planned to enjoy each minute and, when it was over, cherish every memory. It was a temporary happy ending to an unpleasant episode in her life. And Paris was yet to come!

Two days later they flew halfway around the world on the sumptuous private jet Mateo hired. Nibbling on mouth-watering cheese and fruit platters, feeling as if she were lounging at a luxury retreat rather than an aircraft, Bailey was certain she would never view air travel the same again.

It was early evening when they landed at Charles de Gaulle. The weather was cool in the City of Light, but the darkening sky held no threat of rain or sleet. Bailey tugged Natalie's silk-lined designer jacket higher around her ears and, loving the chilly nip on her nose—so different from the warm weather in Australia this time of year—slid into the back of the chauffeur driven limousine, with Mateo entering behind her. She guessed her mother would have felt just as excited when she'd arrived in this famous city years before.

As the driver performed a pared down city tour, she lapped up the scenery while Mateo pointed out noteworthy spots. The iconic spire of the Eiffel Tower, the history effused Arc de Triomphe. Then they passed the Louvre and the Pyramid.

Bailey sighed. "I wonder if there's a person in the world who doesn't want to see the *Mona Lisa.*"

His hand found hers and squeezed. "We'll spend an entire day there."

"Before or after we've spent a morning strolling along the Seine? And I want to sip coffee at a gorgeous sidewalk café and gaze up at the obelisk at the Place de la Concorde."

Mateo nuzzled her hair. "We'll do it all. I promise."

They checked into one of the best hotels in the city, only steps from the Champs-Elysees. Bailey held her pounding heart as she took in magnificent glittering chandeliers, mirror polished floors, classic marble statuettes and fountains of fresh scented flowers. She wasn't interested in being wealthy. Money did *not* buy happiness—ask her father. But this kind of experience was different. It was about appreciating another culture. About absorbing history. Enriching one's life by seeing how others communicated and lived. This hotel was a prime example of crème de la crème. Tomorrow they would move among the less fortunate…children without family or homes of their own. Children who lived as Mateo had once done.

As Mateo checked in at the reception desk, Bailey absorbed his effortless sophisticated air. Calling into that orphanage each year must be a bittersweet experience. Were his memories of that place still sharp or were those long ago days more like a dream…as these days would no doubt be to her in a few years' time?

When they reached their suite, Bailey drifted toward a twinkling view, visible past a soaring window, while Mateo wasted no time coming up behind and enfolding her in his arms.

"It's said that Paris in daytime is only resting," he murmured against her hair. "That the city only comes to life at night. So," his breath felt warm on the sweep of her neck, "are you ready to take on the town?"

"I'd love to say yes, but I need sleep." And she didn't want to be dead on her feet tomorrow when they reached their first and most important destination—the orphanage.

"Hungry then?" He twined her arms around his and pressed her extra close. "Or perhaps we ought to check out that fine piece of furniture."

Eyes drifting closed, she hummed out a grin. He meant that canopied bed.

Turning her back on the view—on the glittering spectacle of Paris at night—she rotated until they were facing one another then gifted his stubbly jaw with a lingering kiss.

"I like that idea," she murmured. "Let's freshen up first."

"Only if we do it together."

He led her through to a marble finished room, featuring a classic clawfoot tub, big enough for two. After kissing her thoroughly, a toe-curling taste of what was to come, he left to order up refreshments.

Floating, Bailey ran the gold gooseneck faucet, added salts and bubble liquid into the rising water then, humming, twirled her hair up and set it with a single pin. After stripping off her shoes and Natalie-sponsored clothes, she threaded her arms through an oversized courtesy robe but stopped when she caught her reflection in the window.

Holding her fluttering stomach, she wanted to imprint this precise moment…this dreamlike feeling…into her memory forever. Beyond that pane, Paris was buzzing with music and laughter and life. Even more amazing, beyond that door, Mateo Celeca was looking forward to sharing this bath with her.

Tying the robe's sash, she lowered onto the edge of the bath's porcelain rim and took stock.

Two weeks ago she'd been near desperate to get home,

for the chance to start again. Two weeks ago she'd thought constantly about her father…reliving those earlier happier years…regretting that their relationship had come unstuck. When she'd seen Damon Ross in the city during that exhausting second day back in Australia, her heart had screamed out for her to walk over. To give them another chance. The cab's timely arrival had put a stop to that idea, thank heaven, because there was nothing she could say that she hadn't said before. Nothing she could do that would mend those flattened fences. She'd tried in the past, over and again. The more she'd persisted, the more her father had only wanted to push her away.

One day, perhaps, they'd talk again, Bailey decided, swirling a hand through the deepening warm bubble-filled pool. But that couldn't happen until she'd proven herself to herself. She was young. With the right attitude she could accomplish anything. Go anywhere.

Right now, however, she wanted to help Mateo accomplish his goals here in France. Of course, she also wanted to enjoy this time they had here as lovers. Still, she was mindful of keeping this whirlwind romance in perspective. It would be ridiculously easy to fall in love with an amazing man like Mateo Celeca only to be left behind.

After this time together, that he was so successful and she was so definitely not didn't worry her so much. His state of mind, as far as commitment was concerned, did. She'd briefly wondered whether he might want to find a wife and adopt that little boy he'd spoken about. But Mateo was married to his career and wanted to keep it that way. He'd confessed he was too busy for a family of his own. Too selfish.

Despite his mansion back home and all his lavish possessions, she couldn't believe he was self-centered. Although Mateo kept him well hidden, the orphaned boy he'd once been was still there deep inside. The boy who'd had no one and nothing. She felt the bracelet heavy on her wrist and smiled softly. People had different ways of dealing with the past.

The adjoining door fanned open and Bailey, brought back, pushed herself to her feet. Mateo entered the room carrying a silver service tray holding two champagne flutes and a dish of sliced pear. At the sight of him, the tips of her breasts tingled and her blood instantly heated. But for the white serving cloth draped over his forearm, he was naked.

Her gaze drank him in...tall, toned and completely comfortable in his own gorgeous bronzed skin.

"I hope you didn't answer the door to room service dressed like that," she said, holding off tightening her robe's sash.

"I doubt they'd bat an eye."

With his gaze lidded and hot, he sauntered closer. After placing the tray on a ledge next to the bath, he poured the champagne then handed over a flute. The glasses pinged as they touched.

"To Paris," he said.

"To Paris," she agreed and sipped.

As the bubbles fizzed on her tongue then slid down her throat, Mateo selected the largest piece of pear, bit in and watched juice sluice down his thumb.

"Delicious," he said and licked his lips.

He offered her a taste. But when she moved to take a bite, he lowered the fruit and touched the piece to the hollow of her throat, drawing a calculated circle before sliding the pear farther down.

Pulse rate climbing, Bailey closed her eyes and waited for the cool to glide between the dip of her cleavage, under the folds of her robe. Instead Mateo lowered his head and sucked at the juice slipping a single line down her throat.

Soaking up each and every thrilling sensation, Bailey sighed and let her neck rock back.

As his mouth slid lower, the sash at her waist was released. A moment later, cool air feathered over her exposed breasts, her thighs, at the same time a big palm trailed the plane of her quivering belly then higher, over her ribs and tender swell of each breast.

He nipped her lower lip and spoke of the near overflowing tub. "That bath needs attention."

Winding her arms around his neck, she whispered in his ear, "Me first."

Nine

Although the morning was far too fresh to leave the top down, Mateo arranged a late model French convertible for the road trip.

From Bailey's wide-eyed expression as they cruised beyond the city limits, she was in thrall of the unfolding country scenes…roads lined with trees whose leaves had been kissed with the russets and reds of autumn and far-reaching vineyards busy with the business of harvest. She marveled at the *colombage* houses with their geometric half-timber patterns. Mateo had obliged when she'd begged to stop at a rustic farmhouse with a leaded-glass feature that highlighted a coat-of-arms on the lintel above.

And there was so much more ahead of them.

He didn't dwell on the niggling doubts that had surfaced since she'd accepted his invitation to join him on this trip, although at times he had found himself wondering if he'd acted too quickly—whether he was a fool believing Bailey was cut from a different cloth than Linda. But they were here now, and he intended for them both to make the most of it.

"After we visit the children," Mateo said, stepping on the gas, "we'll go back to Paris and spend a couple of days. Longer if you want."

"Two days will be wonderful," Bailey said, focused on a tractor trundling over a patchwork of fields. "I told Natalie I'd be back on deck by next Monday."

"She won't mind—"

"I know she wouldn't," Bailey said, looking over at him, "but I've taken up enough slack. Natalie was good enough to offer me a job. I need to step up to the plate."

Changing down gears to take a bend, Mateo was deep in thought. That Natalie had offered Bailey a job didn't bother him in the least. What did rankle was the fact that she scrubbed floors to pay back money he would never miss. After the time they'd spent together, the intimate moments they'd shared, if he didn't know that she'd argue, he'd tell her to forget the debt. He'd much rather set her up in an apartment and, if she followed through with the idea, finance her way through university, like Ernesto had done for him.

Of course he'd be clear that any arrangement would not include a marriage proposal. From what she'd told him of her experience with Emilio Conti, she'd be glad of the clarification. She'd had one close call. She wouldn't be looking forward to the sound of wedding bells.

That made two of them. He liked children but he did not want the responsibility of bringing his own into this world. Life was too uncertain. No one could convince him otherwise.

They reached the town by eleven. Five minutes later, the convertible made its way up the long dirt ruts that led to the Ville Laube Chapelle, a fine example of early French architecture which had been restored over time and transformed into a children's home last century. Bailey sighed, taking in the hundred-foot steeple and angels carrying the instruments of Passion adorning the ornamental gables. Unpolished strong buttresses contrasted with the intricate foliage friezes and elevated stained-glass windows that captured then speared back the sun's late morning light.

Mateo's throat thickened enough he had to clear it. So many years on and still, whenever this scene greeted him, he was six again…feeling uncertain again.

As they parked and slid out from the car, a girl with short-cropped, blond hair, standing beneath the enormous oak Mateo remembered, gawped, dropped her skipping rope and raced inside. A moment later, children poured out through opened double doors that near reached the sky. Eager women, alternatively clapping hands to order the scattered children and patting down their dresses, followed. One lady, with chestnut hair that bounced on the shoulders of her yellow blouse, hurried to line the children up in the yard. Madame Nichole Garnier, Mateo's contact and current director of the orphanage.

Many girls held bouquets, flowers plucked from the home's gardens or nearby meadow. Every boy had their shoulders pinned back. When the assembly was reasonably quiet, beaming, Madame Garnier swept up to greet her guests.

"Monsieur Celeca, it is wonderful to see you again," she said in French. Light green eyes sparkled as she came forward and kissed him, first on one cheek then the other. She turned to Bailey. "And you've brought a friend."

"Madame Nichole Garnier." Mateo spoke in English, knowing Madame would follow suit. "This is Bailey Ross."

"Mademoiselle Ross."

"Call me Bailey."

Madame held one of Bailey's hands between the palms of her own. "And you must call me Nichole. I'm very happy you are here." Smiling, Madame held Bailey's gaze a moment longer before releasing her hand and speaking again with Mateo. "The children have been eager for your arrival." She pivoted around and beckoned a boy standing at the middle front of the group: six or seven years of age, dark hair and chocolate brown eyes fringed with thick lashes.

Mateo's chest swelled as he smiled.

Remy.

After Remy strode forward then pulled up before them, Nichole placed her hand on the boy's crown. "You remember Remy, Monsieur."

Mateo hunkered down. He'd hoped that, since last time, someone might have seen the same special qualities and warmth *he* saw in this child. He'd hoped that Remy would have found two people who would love and adopt him. Still, in another sense, he'd looked forward to seeing him again. From the boy's ear to ear grin, Remy hadn't forgotten him either.

"*Bonjour,* Remy," Mateo said.

The boy's mop of hair flopped over his eyes as he smiled and nodded several times. Then, without invitation, Remy reached and took Mateo's hand and Mateo's heart melted more as he was dragged off. He hated whenever he left, but he really ought to come more often.

Bailey looked on, feeling the connection, subtle yet at the same time unerringly strong. These two—Mateo and Remy—had a history. An ongoing solid relationship. When Natalie had suggested Mateo might bring home a child, was she speaking of anyone in particular? Did the Ramirezes know about this boy?

His little hand folded in a much larger one, Remy drew Mateo nearer the other children, still lined up and standing straight as pins. Bailey fogged up watching the girls hand over their flowers and the boys beam as they shook their benefactor's hand.

Exhaling happily, Nichole folded her arms.

"We so look forward to his visits."

"How long has Mateo been coming back?"

"This will make eight years. Two years ago he helped with dormitory renovations. Last year he sponsored the installation of a computer network and fifty stations. This year I'd hoped to discuss excursions. Perhaps, even an extended stay in Paris for the older ones."

Bailey was certain he'd like that idea.

Her gaze ran over the remarkable building that looked something like a smaller version of Notre Dame, without the gargoyles. How many stories those walls must hold.

"Has this place changed much since Mateo's time?" Bailey asked.

"The structure has been renovated many times over the centuries. Some of the furniture and facilities will have been upgraded since Mateo's time, much of it via his own pocket."

Bailey studied the children again, well dressed, obviously well fed, not a one looking discontent. The word orphanage brought up such Dickensian images...never enough food, never enough care or love. But Bailey didn't feel that here. She only felt hope and commitment.

When Mateo had greeted each child, Remy still stood beside him, a mini-me shadow.

"Remy seems quite attached to Mateo," Bailey pointed out.

"I think Mateo is quite attached to *him*." But then Nichole rubbed her arms as if she were suddenly cold. "Remy lost his mother when he was three," she confided in a lowered voice. "His father dropped him here saying he would return when he could. Four years on..." She shrugged.

No sign of him.

Bailey's chest tightened. At least she'd had her mother until she was fourteen. Had a father too, although he'd been emotionally absent these later years. But looking at that little boy...

Bailey angled her head. "Remy seems happy enough. Lively."

Was it because he was too young to fully understand there was another way to live...with a family, a mother and father?

"He's a joy." Then Nichole hesitated. "Although he doesn't speak often. There's nothing wrong with his hearing. Seems he simply doesn't care to talk most of the time." Her expression softened. "But he and Mateo have a relationship that extends beyond words."

A thought struck and Bailey's smile wavered. "Do you think Remy's father will ever come back for him?"

"I can only say Remy will always have a home here if he doesn't."

Nichole Garnier meant it as a comfort but Bailey heard a dirge rather than a choir. From the little she'd seen, this establishment was well run, with genuine carers who were dedicated to their work. Still, any comprehending child would rather be with his parents in a real home if there were any way, even if that father had once abandoned him...wouldn't he?

Hand cupped to his mouth, Mateo called out.

"Bailey, the girls want to meet you. The boys too."

Laughing, Mateo ruffled Remy's hair and Bailey and Nichole moved forward.

"Have you known Mateo long?" Nichole asked as they walked together and bands of birds warbled nearby.

"Not very."

"He's a good man."

Bailey grinned. "I keep hearing that." She'd even said it herself.

"He gives others so much joy. He deserves every happiness."

Bailey heard the tone in Nichole's voice…the suggestion theirs might be a relationship that could bloom into love and marriage. Perhaps she ought to set the older woman straight. She and Mateo might be lovers, but that didn't translate into anything permanent. He didn't *want* anything permanent.

As they met again and Mateo took her hand and introduced her, Bailey reaffirmed to herself—right now, she didn't want permanent either.

After the children dispersed, Nichole Garnier showed them around the buildings and grounds.

Although the kitchen facilities, plumbing and sleeping quarters were all twenty-first century, the exterior was undoubtedly restored medieval; and the interior, including the lower chapel, retained much of its original decoration, including intricate paintings. Having grown up in a young country like Australia, Bailey was in awe of the sense of history these children were surrounded by every day. The hallowed atmosphere made her feel insignificant, humbled, and at the same time part of the very heart of this sacred place, as if she, herself, might have strolled these soaring halls in a former time.

They enjoyed a lunch of soupe a l'oignon and quiche aux legumes after which the children sang for their adult audience. Although she understood little, Bailey couldn't remember a performance she'd enjoyed more. At the concert's close, she and Mateo provided a standing ovation while the children all bowed and grinned.

Mateo had a meeting with Nichole in the afternoon, so Bailey spent time with the children playing escargot—a French version of hopscotch—and le loup and cache-cache, or hide and seek. One little girl, Clairdy, stole her heart. Only five, Clairdy had white blond hair and the prettiest violet colored eyes. She never stopped chatting and singing and pirouetting. By the end of the afternoon, Bailey's stomach ached from laughing and her palms were pink from applauding.

For dinner they gathered in the dining hall. When Nichole said a prayer before the meal, Bailey's awareness of her surroundings swelled again and, from beneath lowered lashes, she studied her company, particularly the man seated beside her. How amazing if she could see all the world with Mateo. Even more incredible if, in between, they could stay here together in France.

Bailey bowed her head and laughed at herself.

If fairy tales came true…

After the meal, she and Mateo said good-night to the children, Madame Garnier and the others, saying they would be back the next day, then slipped outside and back into the convertible. As they drove down those same dirt ruts, Bailey searched her brain. At no time had Mateo discussed where they would be staying.

"Have you booked a room in town?" She asked, rubbing her gloved hands, relishing the car's heat.

"I own a property nearby."

"Well, it can't be the Palace of Versailles," she joked, thinking of his three story mansion in Sydney. But he didn't comment, merely smiled ahead at the country road, shrouded in shadows, stretching out ahead.

Within minutes, Mateo pulled up in front of a farmhouse, similar to the one they'd stopped to study earlier that day. With the car's headlights illuminating the modest stone facade, Bailey did a double take. No immaculate grounds. No ornate trimmings. This dwelling was a complete turnaround from Mateo's regular taste.

As Mateo opened her car door and, offering a hand, assisted her out, Bailey slowly shook her head, knocked off balance.

"We're staying here?"

"You don't like it?" he asked, as he collected their bags.

"It's not that. In fact..." Entranced, she moved closer. "I think it's wonderful." She had only one question. "Does it have electricity?"

"And if it didn't?"

"Then it must have a fireplace."

"It does, indeed." His smile glowed beneath a night filled with stars as they walked to the door.

"In the bedroom?" she asked, imagining the romantic scene.

"Uh-huh."

She studied his profile, so regal and strong. "You never stop surprising me."

At the door, he snatched a kiss. "Then we're even."

A light flicked on as they moved inside and unwound from their coats. The room smelled of lavender and was clean—he must have had someone come in to tidy up—with a three seater settee, a plain, square wooden table and two rattan backed chairs. Bailey's sweeping gaze hooked on the far wall and she let out a laugh.

"There's a fireplace in here too."

He'd disappeared into a connected room, reemerging now minus their bags. Crossing over, he stopped long enough to brush his lips over hers before continuing on and finding matches on the mantel.

"Let's get you warmed up."

Feeling warmer already, she unraveled the scarf from around her neck while taking in the faded tapestries on the walls as well as the flagstone floor, hard and solid beneath her feet. Feeling as if she'd stepped into another dimension—another time—she fell back into the settee and heeled off her shoes.

"How long have you owned this place?"

"I stayed here the first year," he said, hunkering down before the fireplace. "I came back and bought it soon after."

She hesitated unbuttoning her outer shirt. "Eight years ago?"

He'd struck a match. His perplexed expression danced in the flickering shadow and light as he swung his gaze her way.

"Why so surprised?"

"Why haven't you pulled it down and built something more your style?"

When his brows pinched more than before he turned and set the flame to the tinder, Bailey's stomach muscles clenched. She wasn't certain why, but clearly she'd insulted him. He was all about working hard to surround himself with fine things. Possessions that in some way made up for being cast off with nothing as a child. She'd have thought that here, next door to the heart of those memories, his need for material reassurance would be greatest. It was obvious from Madame's testimony and the well-equipped state of the orphanage that Mateo wanted those children to benefit from pleasant surroundings.

Still, whatever she'd said, she didn't want it to overshadow the previous mood.

"I'm sorry," she said, curling her chilled feet up beneath her legs.

"No need to be," he replied, throwing the spent match on the pyre. "You're right."

Finding a poker, he prodded until the flames were established and the heat had grown.

"I had planned to build something larger," he said, strolling back toward her. "But after I spent a few nights under this roof, I found I didn't want to change a thing. In some ways I feel more at home here than I do in Sydney."

Not so odd, Bailey thought as he settled down beside her. Roots and their memories run deep.

His gaze lowered to her hands. Holding up her wrist, he smiled. "Do you know you play with this bracelet whenever you're uncertain?"

Studying the gold links and charms—a teddy bear, a heart, a rainbow—she shrugged. "I didn't know, but I guess it makes sense."

He rotated her wrist so that the flames caught on the gold and sent uneven beams bouncing all over the room. Bailey moved closer. The heat of his hand on her skin was enough to send some of her own sparks flying.

"I've never seen you with it off your arm," he said.

"My mother put it together for me. A charm for each birthday."

Lowering her wrist, he searched her eyes.

"Until you were fourteen?" he said. *Until the year your mother died.*

"I knew about the bracelet all those years before. It was supposed to be my sweet-sixteen gift. But then Dad refused to give it to me, so…"

"You took it anyway?"

"*No.* This bracelet belonged to me but I would never have taken it without my father's consent. When my sixteenth birthday came and went, I begged for him to give it to me. It was a connection…a link to my mother that I'd waited for all that time. He said he wasn't certain I could look after it, but he didn't have the right to keep it from me."

"He gave it to you in the end."

"He never really spoke to me again after that."

"Sounds as if you both miss her very much. You'd have a lot of memories you could share."

She huffed. "You tell him that."

"Why don't you?"

"He wouldn't listen."

"You've tried?"

"Too many times."

He sat back, absorbed in the crackling fire. After a time, he said, "I'd give anything to speak with my biological father."

"What would you say?"

He thought for a long moment and then his eyes narrowed.

"I'd ask him *why*. But I'll never have the opportunity." He found her gaze again. "What would you say to your father if you could?"

She pondered the question as she never had before.

"I guess I'd ask why too."

"One day you'll have your answer."

When she shivered he wrapped his arms around her, bringing her close to the comfort of his natural warmth. His breath stirred her hair.

"Is that better?"

Looking up into his eyes, she spoke from her heart. "Everything's always better when you hold me."

When his brow furrowed, Bailey shrank into herself. Despite the atmosphere, she'd said too much. Not that her words were a lie. She'd never meant anything more in her life. She felt safe, protected, in his arms. But the way that admission had come out...

Too heavy. She'd bet that kind of "I can't live without you" talk had got a number of his previous love interests gently bumped away. But it wasn't too late to reshape her confession, to season it with the tone they were both more than comfortable with.

Pressing closer, she skimmed her lips across his sandpaper jaw, then hummed over the full soft sweep of his mouth. "On second thought, I think I need to have you hold me a little closer."

She felt his smile, heard the rumble of approval vibrate through his chest.

"But there's something stopping that," he murmured as his palm cupped her nape and she nuzzled down to find a hot pulse throbbing in his neck.

"What's that?"

"Clothes."

Delicious heat flushed through her. They'd made love so many times these past weeks, she'd lost count. But something about his voice, his touch, tonight went beyond anything that had come before. Every cell in her body quivered and let her know…whatever they shared would never get any better than this.

But this time she wanted to be the one to lead…to tease and control and drive the other insane with want.

She lifted her face to his and let his lips touch hers before she slid away from his hold and stood in the firelight before him.

"You build a good fire," she said.

He sat straighter. "You're warm now?"

"Beyond warm."

She caught the hem of her lighter shirt and drew it up over her head. The heat of the flames kissed her bare back while Mateo's intent gaze scorched her front. Her heartbeat thudding, she reached around and released her bra and let the cups fall from her breasts to the soft-pile rug at her feet. When he tipped forward, her flesh tingled and nipples hardened beneath his gaze.

She could see in his eyes that he wanted to drag her to him…wanted to kiss and taste her as much as she wanted to devour him too. But she didn't go to him. Instead she recalled how he'd entered the hotel suite bathroom the night before, without a stitch on, ready to stroke and tease.

She first released the clasp above the zip of her dress pants then eased the fabric past her hips, down her thighs. As the pants came down, she leaned over, nearer to where he sat and waited. Close enough for him to reach out and touch. When she straightened, only one item of clothing separated her from her birthday suit.

His breathing was elevated now, his chest beneath that black shirt rising and falling in the firelight. She recognized the fiery intent in his gaze. How long would he go before hauling her in?

She edged a step closer and a muscle in his jaw began to jump. When she reached for his hand and set his hot palm low on her belly, he came forward and traced his warm mouth over her ribs. Trembling inside, she drew his hand down over the triangle of silk at the apex of her thighs then slowly, purposefully, back up again. His kisses ran higher, brushing the burning tip of one breast as his touch trailed and fingers twined around the elastic of her panties sitting high on her hips.

Groaning, he nipped her nipple at the same time he dragged the scrap of silk down.

Time melted away when his head lowered and his mouth grazed what a second before her panties had concealed... tenderly and then deeply as he cupped her behind and urged her ever closer. She didn't resist when he lifted her left leg and curled her calf over his broad shoulder. She only knotted her fingers in his hair as he continued to explore, his tongue flicking and twirling at the same time the heat at her core kindled, sparked and caught light.

A heartbeat from flashpoint, she recalled she hadn't wanted to surrender to these burning sensations this soon. Now it was too late. This felt—*he* felt—too good to stop.

As she was sucked into that void, all her muscles locked, the fire raged and, dropping back her head, she gave herself over to the tide and murmured his name.

She was barely aware of being lowered down upon that soft pile rug or Mateo's hard frame lowering on top of her. As the waves began to ease and, sighing, she opened her eyes, she found the wherewithal to smile. He hadn't taken the time to take off even his shirt before he thrust in and entered her, filling her in every sense while whispering French and Italian endearments in her ear.

Her legs twined around the back of his thighs as her palms grazed up the hot, hard plate of his chest. He began to move, long measured strokes that built on that fire again. Each thrust seemed to nudge precisely the right spot as his lips sipped lightly from her brow, her cheek. When he drove in suddenly hard and fast, she gripped his head and pulled his mouth to hers. His tongue probed as his body tensed and burned above her. Then she felt the warm touch of his palm sculpting over her breast, the pad of his thumb circling the nipple before he rolled the bead and she gasped as a bright-tipped thrill ripped through her.

His mouth left hers as he levered up. Amid the flickering shadows she could see his muscles glistening and working as his hips ground against hers. She trailed her fingertips down the ruts of his abdomen. Then, scooping them lower, she fanned his damp belly before she gripped his hips, closed her eyes and moved with him, feeling the inferno growing, wishing this sensation would never end.

When he groaned and stiffened above her—when he thrust another time and never more deeply—she reached, held on to his neck and joined him, leaping off that glorious ledge again.

Ten

Later they moved into the bedroom. While Bailey slipped under the covers, Mateo built a fire before joining her. Wrapped in each other's arms, they didn't wake until after eight. He couldn't let her leave the bed until they made love again.

An hour later, Mateo met Nichole at the orphanage. They plotted a workable scheme for regular excursions to the city and surrounds, the first planned in the spring to visit the Louvre with a weekend stay over at a boardinghouse. Nichole was beyond excited for the children, many of whom had never set foot much beyond this district. With a deep sense of satisfaction, Mateo signed his name to the draft document. Opening the world could be an invaluable experience for any child, with regard to education as well as a sense of self. He should know.

They ended their meeting on another high note. A child—Nichole wasn't obliged to say who at this time—would leave the orphanage today for a new home and bright new future. Mateo left the room wondering…

Could this child be Remy? He would only be happy for him if it was.

Mateo had promised Bailey a trip to the neighboring village where she could soak up more of the rustic atmosphere she enjoyed so much. But when he found her in the large undercover area, she and her company looked so enthralled he didn't have the heart to disturb them. Bailey was playing house with a few of the younger girls, one of them Clairdy, a blond angel who Remy was fond of.

As the girls' conversation and laughter filtered through the cool late-morning air, Mateo rested back against that enormous oak-tree trunk and crossed his arms. This was the place he'd wanted to escape as a child. These were the grounds he still recalled in disturbing abstract dreams at least once a year. And yet, whenever he visited, the longer he stayed, the more difficult it was to walk away. Today— this minute, watching Bailey play with the girls—he felt that contradiction more strongly than ever. He couldn't seem to settle the opposing forces playing tug-of-war in his mind. Memories reminded him how much he'd once wanted to leave this place and yet something else whispered for him now to stay.

This, of course, was absurd. He had a practice, friends, a life back home. Here, at times, he felt almost like a ghost.

Bailey saw him and arced an arm through the air. "Mateo, come over! Clairdy and Eleanor are baking cookies. You could help."

Clairdy and an equally small Eleanor chattered on in French as they rolled and cut play dough then put the tray into their playhouse oven. Mateo smiled. Reminded him of when he'd helped Mama in the kitchen all those years ago.

"What cookies are you baking?" Mateo asked, sauntering over.

"C'est notre recette spéciale," Clairdy said. *It is our special recipe.*

"Remember not to have the oven too hot or the bottoms will burn," he pointed out.

Eleanor immediately pretended to alter a temperature dial.

Clairdy patted her friend on the back and exclaimed, *"Bon travail!" Good job!*

"These two are inseparable," Bailey said. "I've never seen two children get along so well."

Clairdy was tugging Mateo's sleeve. "Would you like to try one, Monsieur?" she said in French.

Mateo leaned down, hands on knees. "Will they need to cool first?"

Clairdy put her hands on her hips and nodded solemnly at the oven before she told Eleanor two minutes longer and then the cookies needed to cool.

Mateo ran a palm down Bailey's back and whispered, "After the cookies, I'll take you into town."

"Perhaps the girls would like to come."

His brows lifted. *No doubt.* But, "If we take these two, they'll all want to go."

Bailey nodded earnestly, as Clairdy had done a moment ago, then said, "We could hire a bus."

He laughed. "Perhaps we could."

"How did things go with Nichole this morning?" she asked turning more toward him. Her blue eyes had never looked more vibrant.

"We worked out an excursion schedule for next year. The older children will go first."

Bailey's chin came down. "But no one will miss out."

"Everyone will get a trip," he assured her.

Happy with that, she maneuvered in front of him then wrapped his arms around her middle. Her head dropped back against his shoulder as she sighed and took in the industrious scene playing out before them. Eleanor was stepping into a fairy costume; Clairdy was handing her glittering silver wings.

Bailey snuggled back more. "I like it here."

"The climate suits you." He grazed his lips near her temple. "Brings out the pink in your cheeks."

"What about my lips?"

Mateo's physical responses climbed to red alert. With the children engrossed in their game, he pulled her around a cozy corner, gathered her snug against him and purposefully slanted his head over hers. She immediately melted against him, making him feel invincible...taller and stronger than that five-hundred-year-old oak. When their lips softly parted, he wanted to forget where they were and kiss her again.

"It's only early," he murmured against her cheek. "Perhaps we should visit home before trekking off for lunch."

She dropped a lingering kiss on the side of his mouth. "Maybe we could stay here and eat with the kids."

Frowning, he pulled back. "Am I losing my charm?"

A teasing glint lit her eyes. "Would that bother you?"

"Only as far as you were concerned."

He cupped those pink cheeks and kissed her slowly, deeply, until all the world was only them and this embrace. She might have thought he was only flattering her but his last remark was sincere. Today, that other world—with its busy office and appointments and investments and antiques—wasn't important. He wanted to think, and feel, only her.

When his lips drew away a second time, her eyes remained closed. Leaning against the stone wall at her back, she hummed over a dreamy smile.

"Perhaps we should stay here forever."

His stomach slowly twisted. Not because he disagreed but because as outlandish and flippant as her suggestion may be, he was attracted to the idea. As far as he and Bailey were concerned, this trip was supposed to be about nothing more than short-term companionship. Was meant to be about acting on physical attraction. This minute physical attraction was dangerously high…but he was feeling something more. Something new. And he wasn't entirely sure what to do with it.

A woman's voice, emanating from around the corner, brought him back. It was one of the caregivers, the auburn-haired Madame Prideux. Bailey obviously heard too. Her dreamy look evaporated a second before she straightened her blouse and patted away the long bangs from her blushing face.

"Is she looking for you?" Bailey whispered.

"No. Eleanor. She wants her to wash up and come to the office."

"Is something wrong?"

Mateo remembered Nichole's comment about a child leaving.

"My guess is," he said, "that this is little Eleanor's lucky day."

They came out from behind the corner. Eleanor was holding Madame Prideux's hand as they walked together toward the main building. Clairdy sat by herself on a miniature kitchen chair. Mateo felt this little girl's jumbled feelings as if they were his own.

"Don't worry, Clairdy," Bailey said. "Monsieur says Eleanor isn't in trouble."

Not understanding, Clairdy gave Bailey a blank look, let out a sigh then spoke in French. Bailey's eyes widened at the words Mama and Papa. Clairdy knew Eleanor wasn't in trouble. To Clairdy's mind her friend was being rewarded for being the best little girl at the orphanage.

Bailey lowered into the second tiny chair and spoke to Mateo. "Is she saying what I think she's saying?"

He nodded. "Nichole explained this morning that a couple, who've been waiting years, have jumped through the final hoop and obtained consent to adopt."

"Eleanor?"

"It would appear so."

They both studied Clairdy watching her friend walk away toward a different tomorrow. And as Mateo's gut buckled and throat grew thick, he was reminded again of all the reasons he loved coming back. And why he hated it too.

Bailey gazed down at the little girl who a moment ago had been bubbling with life. Now Clairdy's tiny jaw was slack and her shoulders were stooped. When she held her tummy and spoke to Mateo, Bailey guessed the ailment. The innocent she was, Clairdy would be happy for Eleanor finding a mother and a father—a mama and a papa—but how could she not also miss her friend? Likely envy her.

"Does Eleanor get to say goodbye to her friends?" Bailey asked as they escorted a pale Clairdy back to the dorms.

"I have no doubt."

"That's something at least. Not that I'm unhappy for Eleanor," Bailey hastened to add. "It just must be so hard on the ones left behind." She examined Mateo's intense expression as they walked. "But you know that better than me."

"There'll be someone for Clairdy too one day."

She read his thoughts—*for them all, I hope*—and had to stop herself before she blurted out, *I wish it could be me.*

But she'd known this child a couple of days. Even more obvious, she was in no position to think about children in that context and hadn't before this moment. But the brave way Clairdy held her head as they strolled up the main path brought a stinging mist to Bailey's eyes. She might have lost her mother but she'd known and loved her for fourteen beautiful years, and, as difficult to understand as he was, her father had never considered putting her up for adoption. Damon Ross cared about his daughter. These past years, he simply hadn't been able to show it.

They were all three entering the nurse's office as Remy showed up, a scuffed football clamped under his arm. When they came out a few minutes later, Remy was still there, waiting to see how Clairdy was. Something older than his years shadowed that little boy's eyes; he knew she needed a friend more than medicine. Remy said a few words to Mateo—something in French, of course. Mateo nodded and Remy took Clairdy's hand and led her upstairs to the girls' dorm to rest.

They both watched until the pair disappeared around the top balustrade. Bailey let out a pent-up breath. She couldn't stop thinking about what her mother would've done in this situation.

"We could stay and read her a story," she suggested and stepped toward the stairs, but Mateo's hand on her arm held her gently back.

"She might like to be alone with Remy now."

Bailey wanted to argue, but it was as much herself as Clairdy she wanted to console. This was a small taste of what Mateo must see each time he visited. There was the fabulous welcome and smiling familiar faces, time set aside to make plans for improvements he knew would be appreciated. But those same faces who were overjoyed to see him couldn't help but be sad when he drove away. He must want to take each and every one of these children home with him, and realizing he couldn't...

Bailey hung her head.

A lesser man might simply send a check.

As they moved away from the building toward that big sprawling tree out front, Mateo circled his arm around her waist. "Let's take a drive."

She hesitated but then nodded. If they went out, talked, her mind, and his, would be taken off a situation over which they had no power. And she had to be happy for Eleanor and pray that Mateo was right. A perfect family was around the corner for Clairdy. Remy too.

Mateo drove over that ancient stone-bridge and into the village with a towering gothic church, two restaurants, one bakery…and right on through.

Bailey shot over a glance. "Where are we going?"

"Thought you might like to see something a little different. A fortress. A ruin now. Word is it's haunted."

Determined not to be sullen, she set her mittened hands in her lap. "I'm in."

After a few more minutes traveling along the country road, they reached the foot of a rocky cliff that jutted over the river. Ascending a series of rock slabs that served as steps, Bailey, with Mateo, reached near the summit a little out of breath. But given their incredible surroundings, she soon forgot her tired legs.

"Nine-hundred-years ago this began as a motte—a large mound—and wooden keep," Mateo told her. "An earlier word for keep is *donjon*."

It clicked. "As in dungeon?"

He winked, took her hand and led her toward the ruins. "By the fifteenth century, the fortress consisted of three enclosures surrounding an updated keep. Only the château of the second enclosure still stands."

Bailey soaked up the sense of history effused in the assorted moss-covered arches, sagging stone steps, the remnants of sculptures hanging to cold gray walls. Above what once must have been an imposing door rested a worn coat of arms. Shading her eyes, she peered up. A giant might have taken a ragged chomp out of the second story wall.

"Who are the ghosts?" she asked. "Why do they haunt?"

"It's said that a lord once kept his daughter locked in this tower. Apparently no man was good enough, but everyone knew the true reason. The lord didn't want to lose his only child." Holding her elbow, he helped her over rubble through to a cool interior that smelled of mold and earth. "Then, one day, a knight rode through and was invited to stay for the evening meal. The knight heard the maiden singing and crying. He asked if he could speak with her. But the lord wouldn't allow it."

Bailey had been picking her way up the stairs. Now she swung around to face him. "Don't tell me they both died while the knight was trying to rescue her?"

"The knight succeeded in freeing his lady and they rode away that night to be wed. The father was furious and set out on horseback to bring his only child back. Taking a jump, his horse faltered and the lord broke his leg. Infection set in. He took six weeks to die, but he moaned and howled for his daughter's return until his last breath. He wanted her forgiveness," he added.

Bailey studied the lonely crumpling walls and coughed out a humorless laugh. "Funny thing is that lord never enjoyed his daughter's company while he had it."

Reading between the lines, Mateo crossed the dirt floor and joined her midway up the steps.

"If you'd like to see your father when we get back," he said, "I'd be happy to go with you."

She cupped his bristled cheek. "Thanks, but I can't see any happy ending there either."

"I'm sure if you gave him a chance—"

"Maybe he should give me one for a change." Gathering herself, she blew out a breath. She didn't want to discuss it. There was no point. "I wish it were different, but it's not."

A muscle in his cheek pulsed as he considered her response.

"I suppose it's not easy."

Bailey frowned. Did he mean for her or her father? How would he handle the situation if he ever became estranged from his child? How would he handle any situation as a father? She wanted to ask. And now seemed the time.

"Natalie mentioned at dinner that night she wouldn't be surprised if one year you came home with a child from France."

His face hardened. "Natalie's sweet but she doesn't have all the facts."

"What are the facts?"

"For a start, nowadays the adoption process in France is a longwinded one."

"So you've looked into it?"

"Madame and I have conversed for many years."

Be that as it may, he hadn't answered the question. "Then you've never considered adopting?"

His voice and brow lowered. "Remy will find a perfect home."

"Maybe it could be with you."

The muscle pulsed again before he headed back down the steps. "It's hard, Bailey, I know, to think about leaving those kids behind. But they're well looked after. I do what I can."

Bailey let out a breath. Of course he did, and far more than most people would. Resigned, she admitted, "It's probably best we're leaving tomorrow or I might never want to go. Those kids have a way of wrapping themselves around your heart."

From the foot of the stairs, he found her gaze. "That's the

way it is. When you have to stay, you don't want to. When you're free to leave..." His gaze dropped away.

That's the way it was for her with Mateo, Bailey realized walking with him back out into the open. When she'd had nowhere to go and Mateo had convinced her to stay to rest up, she'd been intent on leaving. She'd ended up sharing his bed for two weeks then flying with him here. And in these few days she'd become frighteningly used to the sight of him sitting before a flickering fire in their cottage. Used to his earnest evaluating walks around the orphanage, as well as his warm smile when any one of the children brought him a drawing or sang him a song. She felt so *close* to him. As if they'd known each other before.

What would happen when they returned to Australia? She'd be earning her own money...would be free to live her own life. She had no real reason to stay at the Celeca mansion any longer.

Only now she wasn't so keen to go.

Eleven

Mateo looked over the children playing in the late October sunshine and ran damp palms down his trouser legs. He and Bailey had spent three days at the Chapelle. At the end of each day they returned to his stone cottage to talk and make love into the night. The French countryside this time of year, the children's laughter mixed with memories...he didn't want to leave.

Bailey didn't want to go either. If she hadn't seemed so determined to start work again next week, he'd tell her they would stay a few more days. She seemed to fit here among the trees and the quiet.

He wanted to see more of her when they returned to Australia. But he also wanted to be clear on his position. He was not after marriage. Children of his own. If she accepted that, he'd be more than happy to continue what they shared for however long it lasted.

Bailey was strolling along the paved path with Madame

Garnier. Clairdy walked a step behind, looking a little recovered from her news yesterday about her friend leaving. Shoving his hands in his pockets, Mateo headed toward them. All those years ago, he'd been overjoyed when Ernesto had taken him away from here, like his friend Henri had left before him. The friend he'd so love to know again. It hurt to see that little girl's malaise but that's all he could wish for each of these children. That one day soon they would find a family of their own.

A stiff breeze tugged at his coat. He examined the sky. Rain on the way. He should call Bailey now, say their goodbyes and, if they were going, head off.

Bailey and Madame strolled over.

"Are you ready to leave, Monsieur?" Madame asked.

Mateo folded Bailey's gloved hand in his. "We'd best go now or the mademoiselle will miss out on seeing Paris."

Nichole clapped twice, loudly, and children, coming from everywhere, promptly lined up.

"Monsieur Celeca must leave now," Nichole said in French. "Would you all thank him and the mademoiselle for visiting?"

In unison, the children said in French, "Thank you. We will miss you."

But even as Mateo's chest swelled at the sight of so many adoring little faces and their heartfelt words, his gaze skated up and down the line and soon he frowned. One was missing.

"Where's Remy?" he asked.

"Remy is a little under the weather today." Madame reached into a pocket. "He asked that I give you this."

She fished out a handmade card. When Mateo opened the paper, his heart torqued in his chest then sank to his knees.

Don't forget me, Monsieur.

There was a drawing of a smiling boy holding a football.

Mateo groaned, then, setting his jaw, started off. "I'll go see him."

But Madame's firm hand on his arm pulled him up. Her green eyes glistened with sympathy and understanding.

"I think, Monsieur, it is best that you don't. I'll keep an eye on Remy. He'll be fine, I promise."

Mateo held Nichole's gaze for a long tortured moment as his thoughts flew and a fine sweat broke on his brow. She knew that if he went upstairs to Remy he would want to take him. And he *couldn't*. For so many reasons. He had to go and let Remy find a couple who wanted a family. That boy didn't need an overworked, set-in-his-ways bachelor.

After the women and Clairdy hugged, he and Bailey headed to the car, and the children began to sing. Emotion biting behind his eyes, Mateo fought the urge to look back. Seeing out the corner of his eye that Bailey's hands were clenched together, it was all he could do not to. But he was scared that if he did, he would see Remy, standing as *he* had once stood, at a second-story window, wondering if two friends would ever meet again.

Mateo barely spoke the whole drive to Paris. Whenever Bailey tried to make conversation, he answered and that was all.

From the first, she'd been aware of the connection he and Remy shared. Now Mateo felt terrible leaving that little boy behind. More terrible than she felt leaving Clairdy, and that was bad enough. But as Mateo had said, he did what he could. Neither of them was in a position to do any more...even if they desperately wanted to.

Still, she wished she could have the happy, talkative Mateo back again.

As the convertible hurled them ever closer to Paris and away from the Chapelle, Bailey told herself not to dwell on the possibility of Mateo being a father to Remy as Ernesto had been a father to him. Watching farmhouses and fields whiz by, she reminded herself that Mateo had a bachelor lifestyle—a busy career—that didn't correlate with having children. Remy deserved a family who were prepared to give up anything and everything to adopt him. When Mateo flew over next year, Remy might well be gone. And that was best.

Wasn't it?

They checked into the same hotel on the Champs-Elysees and, as if neither of them wanted to dwell on where they had been—how different it felt to be back in the bosom of luxury as opposed to snuggling beneath the patchwork quilt of their stone cottage—they had their bags taken to their suite and immediately set off to sightsee.

As they strolled arm in arm along the Champs-Elysees, Mateo explained, "The people of Paris refer to this avenue as *la plus belle avenue du monde*. The most beautiful avenue in the world."

Bailey had to agree. Finally soaking up the sights she'd heard so much about felt amazing. The atmosphere was effused with so much history and courage and beauty. Every shop and tree and face seemed to greet her as if they were old rather than new friends.

She cupped a hand over her brow to shield the autumn sun from her eyes. "It seems to go on forever."

"Two kilometers. It ends at the Arc de Triomphe, the monument Bonaparte built to commemorate his victories."

They strolled beside the clipped horse-chestnut trees and lamplights, passing cinemas, cafés and so many speciality shops, before stopping for lunch at a café where the dishes marked on a chalkboard menu ranged from sweet-and-sour sea bass and lobster ravioli to more casual fare such as club sandwiches. After taking a seat among the pigeons at one of the many sidewalk tables, Bailey decided on the crab and asparagus salad, while Mateo liked the sound of braised lamb with peaches.

"Is this a favorite café when you're in town?" She asked, sipping a glass of white wine.

"This is my first time eating here."

"Then I think today we've found the perfect place to simply sit and watch."

He raised his glass. "A favorite Parisian pastime. Keeping an eye out for the unique and the beautiful."

Bailey had been watching a pair of young lovers, laughing as they meandered down the avenue. Now her focus flicked back to Mateo and the intense look in his dark eyes made her blush. He wasn't looking at the beautiful view. He was looking at her.

They enjoyed their meal then headed off to the Louvre on the bank of the Seine. Bailey couldn't stop from beaming. So much to take in...over thirty-five thousand works of art dating from antiquity to modern times...Da Vinci, Rubens as well as Roman-Greco and Egyptian art collections...she felt deliciously lost as more and more worlds unfolded before her. She adored Michelangelo's *The Slave* and openly gaped at the *Venus de Milo*. But she fell completely in love with Canova's *Psyche Revived by Cupid's Kiss*.

Cupid's wings were raised behind him, his head slanted over the unconscious Psyche's as he held her close. Bailey was in awe of the depth of emotion the master had captured in marble.

"This is my favorite," she decided. "You can see how in love with her he is."

"Legend has it that Venus was jealous of Psyche's beauty," Mateo said, wrapping his arms around her from behind. "She sent her son, Cupid, to scratch Pysche with an arrow while she slept. When Psyche awoke, she would fall in love with the first man she saw: a hideous creature that Venus planned to plant in the bed. But Cupid woke Psyche and, startled, he accidentally scratched himself as well. Under the arrow's spell, they fell instantly in love."

"And lived happily ever after?"

"They had a spat and Venus put some more obstacles in the way. The last sent Psyche into a dead sleep, that only Cupid's kiss could cure."

She sighed. "Like in *Sleeping Beauty*."

"Like you in the mornings," he murmured against the shell of her ear.

She smiled and admitted, "I'm not the lightest of sleepers."

"Waking you is my favorite time of the day."

He brushed his lips down the side of her throat and the backs of her knees turned to jelly. But she was well aware of their public surroundings.

"You want to get us thrown out."

He chuckled. "We're in *France*."

While Mateo continued to nuzzle her cheek, she thought again of the sculpture and its legend. "What happened at the end of their story?"

"Our old friend Zeus blessed their union and gifted Psyche immortality. She and Cupid had a daughter, Voluptas, the goddess of sensual pleasure."

Bailey's eyes widened. "*Voluptas*. Bet she has a story or two of her own."

Laughing—his old self again—he led her away.

They cruised around the exhibits until the museum closed up at ten. But outside they found the city sparkling and very much awake. Making their way along the Seine, they drank in the river's shimmering reflections and music floating over the cold night air.

He released her hand and drew that arm around her waist. "What would you like to do tomorrow?"

"That's easy." She cuddled in as they walked. *"Everything."*

"In a single day?"

"We have a day and a half," she corrected. "And I put myself entirely in your hands."

"Entirely?"

"And exclusively."

He growled playfully, "I like the sound of that," then turned her in his arms to steal a bone-melting kiss that sparked a wanting fire low in her belly and kept it burning.

They found a warm place to enjoy coffee and share a pastry, then walked again. When dawn broke—a palette of pink and gold soaking across the horizon—cold and worn out, she yawned and couldn't stop.

Mateo raised his hand to hail a cab. "Time to turn in."

"But—"

"No buts," he growled before opening the back passenger door of the cab that had pulled up. "We have another big day coming up."

She didn't like when he was bossy. Even if he was right. Nestled in the back seat, she rested her cheek against his shoulder. Smiling drowsily, she found she couldn't keep her eyes open. As her lids closed, all the sights and sounds and smells of their day in Paris flooded her mind. She snuggled more against his warm hard chest and murmured, "I loved our night. Love it here. I love…*I love…*"

Mateo waited for Bailey to finish. But, with the sun rising—with the full day they'd had—she was asleep before her last words were out. After pressing a kiss on her brow, he too closed his eyes.

When they arrived at the hotel, he roused himself and eased away. But Bailey didn't wake, so he carefully scooped her up in his arms and, entering the lobby, asked the doorman to follow him to an elevator and help him into his suite. A few minutes later, the concierge swiped open the suite's door and, on Mateo's orders, hurried to draw back the bed's covers before bidding him a hushed very good morning.

Searching Bailey's contented face, Mateo carefully laid his sleeping beauty upon the sheets. She stirred when he removed her coat and shoes but after he stripped and lay down to join her, she curled up against him and huddled deeper as he drew the covers up around her chin. His body cried out for rest but he didn't want to give into sleep.

The view was too good.

As he stroked her hair and watched growing light play over the contours of that button nose, the curve of her lips, Mateo's chest grew warm. Despite lingering memories of the Chapelle earlier today, he'd never known this depth of peace. The feeling that he had what he needed to survive, to be happy, was right here with him now in his arms.

He'd mulled it over before. Now his mind was made up. No more wondering if Bailey was anything like his manipulative ex. When they were home again in Sydney, he'd make it official. He would make their current living arrangement more permanent. No contracts. No rings. Just an agreement to share each other's company.

And his bed.

Twelve

At nine the next morning, a soft caress at the shell of Bailey's ear stirred her from her dreams. Smiling, stretching and sighing, she rolled over and remembered where she was and with whom. In Paris with the most incredible man.

Mateo dotted a kiss on her nose, on her cheek.

"You were sleeping soundly." His voice was deliciously husky the way it always was first thing in the morning, and she found herself sighing at her body's reaction to the desire evident in his hooded eyes and slanted smile. Coiling her arms around his neck, she brought his lips to hers while his hot palm trailed up her side. Within seconds her heartbeat was racing.

She couldn't remember the last of that cab ride last night. Couldn't remember how she'd arrived back in this suite. She did know, however, that this minute she felt amazingly snug, wonderfully safe. She remembered their agreement... today she was entirely, exclusively his. How she wanted to pull the covers up over their heads and spend the next few hours in bed.

Reluctantly breaking the kiss, he murmured against her lips. "It's time to get up."

Groaning, she dragged the back of her hand over her tired eyes. *Bossy again.* "What time is it?"

"Time to see Paris."

A second passed when she could have smoothed her fingers over his muscled shoulder and drawn his mouth back to hers. But this was their only full day left in France. She couldn't pass that up, even for such a compelling reason.

With not nearly enough sleep, Bailey was slow to shower and dress. But the moment they were back on the Parisian streets, coats pulled up around their ears, she was bubbling with excitement.

They visited Notre Dame, the legendary home of the hunchback, then went on to an artist's paradise, Montmatre et Sacre Coeur, situated on a hill in the north of Paris. It boasted the famous Moulin Rouge at its base and the famed Sacre Coeur Basilica, with its inspirational equestrian statue of Joan of Arc, at its summit. She made sure Mateo took plenty of snapshots.

After changing for dinner back at their suite, they took the elevator to the top of the Eiffel Tower where they caught the last of the sunset. Gazing over the city's buildings and monuments draped in a coat of gold, Bailey tried to imprint her mind with every inch of the breathtaking panorama. Mateo circled his arm around her waist and handed his camera to a German tourist who ensured the moment was captured.

He thanked the man then asked her, "Are you hungry?"

"I'm starving." They'd had a bagel on the run, but that was hours ago. "What do you have in mind?"

"A special treat."

As they descended, Mateo revealed his biggest surprise of the day. He'd booked well in advance a table at The Jules Verne, one of Paris's most exclusive restaurants, situated on the tower's second floor.

They were shown to a table by a window facing north across the fountains and enjoyed a night of exquisite cuisine, the best of champagne, while surrounded by a glittering blanket of city lights.

When the waiter removed their dessert dishes, Mateo slid a hand across the white linen tablecloth. His fingers folded around hers.

"Did you enjoy the meal?"

"I enjoyed *everything*."

He grinned, and the smile lit his eyes. His index finger had begun to toy with her bracelet's charms...the heart, the bear.... He looked down but then frowned and took a closer look.

"You ought to have that catch checked out. It's near worn through."

Worried, she inspected the clasp then each of the charms to make certain none were missing. "Guess it should be worn. I don't take it off." Bailey's stomach looped and knotted at the thought of losing it. "After so long, I wouldn't feel whole without this around my wrist."

"We'll get a safety chain for it tomorrow."

"I'll look after it when we get home."

Mateo didn't look pleased. But it wasn't his place to insist.

He reached and took her hand again, angling her wrist to study the charms. "Have you added to it since your sixteenth?"

"It's never felt quite right. It'd have to be a really special charm." She didn't own much, but this possession was sacred. Not that her father would understand that. Even now he probably thought she was a day away from harming or losing it.

"What about you?" She asked, looking up from their twined hands; hers looked so small and pale compared to his. "Do you have any childhood mementos hidden away?"

Mateo's gaze grew distant and his brows knitted before he shook his head. "No. Nothing material."

Bailey's heart went out to him. Given all his chattels back in Sydney, that answer made sense.

"But I do have something," he said. "A memory I treasure."

She sat straighter. "Memories are good."

"The day Ernesto came back to the Chapelle for me. It was spring and everyone was playing outdoors. He called me over, beside that old oak and he said, 'Mateo, if you'd like to be my son…'" His Adam's apple bobbed before he seemed to come back from that distant spot. Then he shrugged and gave an offhanded smile. "How's that. I've forgotten the rest."

From the way his dark eyes glistened, she didn't think so. But she understood. Memories were the most valuable of all keepsakes. He was entitled to protect his. He'd certainly given her some amazing memories these past days to cherish.

Leaning closer, she confessed with all her heart, "I'll never forget our time here."

When his gaze darkened more and his jaw jutted almost imperceptibly, Bailey sat back as a shadowy feeling slid through her. They'd shared so much. Seemed to have gotten so close. But was that open admission too much? Had she sounded too much the lovesick schoolgirl?

But then a smile swam up in his eyes and the tension seemed to fall from his shoulders. He lifted her hand, dropped a light kiss on the underside of her wrist and murmured against her skin, "I won't forget either."

After dinner they strolled again, but the weather had turned even chillier and, while they'd been lucky so far, Bailey smelled rain on the way. She tried her best but when she couldn't keep her teeth from chattering, Mateo stopped to turn and envelope her in his coat-clad arms.

"I'll take you back to the suite," he said.

Her heart fell. "I don't want to go in yet."

"We can always come back."

Come back? She searched his eyes. Was she reading him right? "You mean...to France?"

"And sooner than I usually plan."

Bailey couldn't take a breath. It was a generous, wonderful offer but...should she read more into it? She supposed she ought to ask herself, *How much more did she want?* They'd been sleeping together, enjoying each other's company, but did she want a relationship, *if* that's what he was saying?

Her smile quavered at the corners as she tried to contain her whirling mix of emotions. As they headed for a cab stand, she smiled a jumpy smile and said, "I'd like that."

Thirteen

Mateo made love to Bailey that night feeling both content and never more conflicted. Caressing her silken curves as they played upon the sheets...kissing every sensual inch of her and only wishing there were more. He couldn't deny that he wanted to keep this woman in his life even if, with every passing hour, he felt himself treading farther into dangerous ground.

After the Emilio affair, it was safe to presume Bailey wasn't interested in exchanging vows and wedding bands. He'd invited her back to Paris and she'd agreed. Would she presume, too, that he would also invite her to live under his roof on a more permanent basis? In time, would she expect more? Deeper commitment?

Diamond rings?

Mateo slept on the problem and when they stepped out to bid the City of Light good morning, with Bailey looking so vibrant and fresh on his arm, he made a decision—one he hoped she would be happy with. But now wasn't the time to discuss it.

He arranged for them to spend the morning on a cruise, absorbing the sights from a different point of view. They boarded near the Pont-Neuf Bridge.

"Its name literally means the new bridge," Mateo said as they settled into window seats beneath a Perspex roof that allowed an unhindered view of the sights, including the many graceful arches of the stone bridge. "But this is the oldest bridge in Paris."

Bailey narrowed her gaze on a distant point then tipped forward. "Look there."

She pointed out a couple standing at the center of this side of the bridge in the midst of a passionate kiss. Before their lips parted, the man swept the woman up in his arms and twirled her around. They were both laughing, bursting with happiness.

Bailey melted back into her seat. "I bet he just proposed."

Mateo's chest tightened at her words, at her tone. Shifting, he got comfortable again and explained, "The *Pont-Neuf* is rumored to be one of the most romantic places in the city."

She laughed. "Is there anywhere in Paris that *isn't* romantic?"

He gave an honest reply. "Not this trip."

All expression seemed to leech from her face before she blushed...her cheeks, her neck. From the look, she'd gone hot all over. That made him smile but also made him want to pull back. He really ought to rein it in. Although she knew his mind on the subject, he didn't want to confuse the issue. Companionship was good. A marriage proposal was not.

After a leisurely time enjoying the sights from the river, he helped her off the boat. Her posture and thoughtful look told him she wasn't looking forward to leaving this behind and boarding that jet. But he had one more surprise before they left. One that would, hopefully, surpass all the others.

As they meandered along the avenue, she said, "Suppose we'd better get back to the suite and pack."

He kept a straight face. "I need to duck in somewhere first."

"Souvenir shopping?"

He twined her arm around his. "In a way."

He hailed a passing cab. When they arrived at their destination, Bailey didn't seem able to speak. Her eyes merely sparkled, edged with moisture, as she clasped her hands under her chin.

"It didn't seem right that we leave without visiting here," he said, stepping out from the cab.

"The Paris Opera," she breathed.

"I have tickets, but the matinee starts soon." He extended his hand to help her out. "Let's hurry."

He escorted her toward a magnificent facade adorned with numerous towering rose-marble columns. The highest level was bookended by two large gilded statues. The interior luxury, including mosaic covered ceiling and multiple chandeliers, had been compared to the corridors in Versailles. When Bailey spotted the 98-foot high marble grand staircase—the one his own was based on—she gasped and held her throat. As he took her arm and escorted her up the flight, she looked over and beamed.

"I don't need a ball gown or glass slippers. No one could feel more like Cinderella than I do now."

When they emerged from the theater, she was floating. She literally couldn't feel her feet descending those incredible grand stairs. The performance was a thoroughly beautiful ballet Bailey knew she would dream about for months.

As they made their way toward the exit, all those amazing

sparkling chandeliers lighting their way, Mateo checked his watch.

"We have a little time yet before we need to head off to the airport. What would you like to do?"

She remembered a mention of souvenirs earlier and piped up. "Buy a gift."

"Who for?"

"I wanted to get Natalie something to thank her for taking me on then letting me have this week off. But then I thought she'd appreciate something for Reece far more."

Chuckling, he wound her arm more securely around his. "You're right. She would."

"Maybe some kind of stuffed toy. A Gallic Rooster." Her step faltered at his unconvinced look. "It's this country's national animal, isn't it?"

"But Reece isn't a baby. He'd appreciate something more—" he thrust out his chest "—masculine."

She slanted her head. Okay. "How about a football?"

"Too young."

"Suggestion?"

"That we go to the experts."

"And that would be?"

He quickened his step and propelled her along with him. "The oldest and largest toy store in Paris."

Soon they arrived at Au Nain Bleu, the massive store that had been serving French children's play needs since the mid-nineteenth century. There were lots of stuffed floppy-eared rabbits. Bailey seemed especially taken with a pair of bunny slippers. But Mateo ushered her through to a spot where boys' toys ruled.

They looked at trucks, action figures, miniature drums. Bailey drifted toward a nearby girls' section while Mateo kept searching. After a few more minutes, satisfied, he called and gestured toward a shelf.

Bailey hurried over from a jewelry stand and picked up the pack. "A builder's kit, suitable for eighteen months to three years," she said. With a plastic hammer, automatic wrench, an "electric" drill that buzzed when you pressed a red button. "But Reece is only twelve months."

"Believe me, he'll grow into it quickly."

She quizzed Mateo's eyes and smiled.

"You would have liked this when you were young?"

"More than anything, I wanted to be a builder."

"And you ended up becoming a doctor?"

"Ernesto wanted me to make the most of my grades."

She smiled knowingly. "But there's still a part of you that wants to hammer and saw and create."

He rolled that thought over and admitted, "I suppose there is." Although he hadn't thought about it in decades. He straightened his shoulders. "Anyway, I'm sure you'll be a hit with Reece with this."

At the counter, Mateo pulled out his wallet but Bailey held up a hand. "I have money enough for this."

He wanted to argue but finally put his wallet away while she extracted some French currency. He hadn't known she'd exchanged any cash. But given her backpacker history, of course she'd be well up to speed on such things.

The lady behind the counter insisted on gift wrapping. Mateo was checking his watch again as they headed for the exit when a large well-dressed man materialized directly in front of them. With a stony expression, he studied Bailey who, looking uncertain, slid a foot back. Mateo wasn't uncertain. He was annoyed. They had a jet to catch.

Before Mateo had a chance to speak up, the man addressed Bailey in French.

"I am a security officer for the store. Please empty your pockets."

Bailey clung to his arm. "What's he saying?"

Mateo stepped in front of Bailey and demanded of the officer, "What's this about?"

"I have reason to suspect your wife has something in her pocket for which she did not pay."

Bailey's hushed voice came from behind. "Why is he upset, Mateo?"

He looked over his shoulder. "He thinks you've shoplifted."

Her eyes rounded. "That's crazy."

Yes. It was.

And yet he couldn't help but wonder why a security officer from a well reputed store should stop them if there was no basis to the accusation.

Stepping beside her again, Mateo assessed her knee-length coat. "He wants you to empty your pockets."

"What on earth does he think I stole?"

"The quickest way to end this, Bailey, is show him the contents of your pockets."

If she had nothing to hide, she would have nothing to fear and, doing his job or not, he would then demand an apology from this man. If, of course, the security guard was right...

As shoppers swirled around them and a toddler, trying a mini slide, squealed close by, Bailey reluctantly dragged something shiny from her right pocket then held out her hand, palm up. The officer preened his moustache before leaning in to take a better look. Mateo didn't need to. He knew what Bailey had hidden in her pocket.

The officer angled his head and frowned. "What is this?"

Sheepish, Bailey found Mateo's eyes. "You were right. The clasp broke when I was looking through a display. It fell in with some necklaces. I put it in my pocket and was going to have it fixed, first thing, when we got home."

Mateo let out a lungful of air. Her charm bracelet. She was lucky she hadn't lost it. He knew how much it meant to her. He should have *made* her listen.

Mateo explained the situation to the officer who accepted the story with an apology before allowing them to be on their way.

"I know what you're thinking," she said as they walked out onto the pavement. "It could have slipped off without me knowing." She cringed. "I hate to think what my father would say."

"He wouldn't be happy."

"I'm used to that. But you don't need to be upset."

He didn't reply.

As they cabbed it back to the suite, Mateo mulled over the incident. What really bothered him was that for a moment he'd been prepared to think the worst of Bailey—again. But it had been a misunderstanding, something similar to when he'd jumped to conclusions the second she'd confirmed she'd taken that money from Mama. But that hiccup was long behind them. Bailey wasn't dishonest. Wasn't manipulative.

He stole a glance at her profile as she watched the Parisian streets flash by in her borrowed designer clothes, perhaps thinking of her visit to the Champs-Elysees, and confirmed she wasn't that type. She couldn't be.

He couldn't feel this deeply about someone who was nothing better than a fraud.

Or, more correctly, he couldn't make that mistake again.

They packed, checked out and boarded the jet with time to spare. Bailey felt as if she were grieving for a friend as she gazed out the window, bid goodbye to France and the jet blasted off. She felt as if she were leaving home, leaving her family—Nichole and the children at the orphanage.

Mateo had said they would visit again, and she was over the moon about that. But now, more than before, she also needed to know what would happen to "them" when they arrived back in Australia.

As the jet climbed higher and clouds began to interfere with the view of the receding ground below, she considered hedging around the subject, trying to get an answer without sounding needy or obnoxious by asking directly. Because she hadn't the money to find her own place and wanted to pay that loan back as quickly as she could, she'd agreed to live at Mateo's home...his *mansion*.

But as close as she believed they'd become—as close as she'd come to acknowledging feelings she'd been determined to stay away from less than three weeks ago—she had to know where they were in their...well, their *relationship*. She couldn't land in Sydney and simply walk through his front door as if she owned the place. She needed to know what the next step was, and the best way was to ask straight out.

She set her magazine aside. "You know, with the wage I'll make cleaning, I should have that loan paid back in a couple of weeks."

He looked across, smiled. "That's great."

When he looked back at his obstetrician periodical, she folded her hands firmly in her lap. Since that incident at the toy store, he'd seemed distracted. A silly part of her wondered if, for just a second, he might have believed the security buffoon's accusation. But she hadn't pilfered a thing in her life. He might have set out thinking she'd shammed his grandmother but surely, after the week they'd spent together, he knew her by now. She'd even begun to think that he might be falling a little in love with her. That left her feeling dizzy and, perhaps, even a bit hopeful.

She shook herself. This mooning wasn't getting her any closer to finding out what came next. If either of them truly *wanted* a next.

She drummed four fingertips on the magazine page. "I thought I should start shopping for a place to live before then."

He froze then lowered the periodical and studied her eyes. "Do you want to find a place of your own?"

Bailey swallowed a fluttery breath. What kind of question was that? What kind of reply did she give? Honest, she supposed.

"Depends. Do you want me to?"

His gaze dropped to her hands and again she realized how naked she felt without that bracelet on her wrist. She was squirming a little when he announced, "I thought you might like to stay with me."

Her entire body lit with a blush. She coughed out a laugh, shrugged, tried to find words while attempting to sort out if she really did want to "live with a man" so soon after her pseudo engagement catastrophe, even if that man was the uber attractive, thoroughly irresistible, Mateo Celeca.

Bowing her head, she let out a shuddery breath. This was a thousand times different from Italy. She and Mateo had a connection, something she wanted to pursue…if he did.

She took a breath and looked him in the eye. "Are you sure?"

He waited two full beats where Bailey could only hear her heart pounding in her ears. Then he leaned close, stroked her cheek and murmured against her lips.

"I'm sure."

Fourteen

A week later, Bailey sat at the meals table next to Mateo's chef-standard kitchen. She'd been struggling all morning with a question. A problem. Finally now she'd made up her mind.

She pushed her coffee cup away and announced, "I'm going to do it."

Sitting alongside of her, Mateo shook out his Sunday paper, looked over and announced, "Fabulous." Then he frowned and asked, "Do what?"

Bailey let her gaze roam the hedges and statues in her favorite of Mateo's gardens—the one that reminded her so much of their time in France—then she studied the bracelet, repaired and back on her wrist. Her stomach turned and she swallowed the lump formed in her throat.

"I'm going to see my father."

The day after they'd returned, she'd gone back to work, cleaning for Natalie's firm; she'd decided to keep Reece's gift until she and Mateo saw them all together. He'd put the rest of his vacation plans on hold and seemed content to play golf and catch up with local friends. He'd said that seeing as Mama hadn't expected him, she wouldn't be disappointed and that he'd visit her and Italy sometime soon. Every night they came together but, although the words almost escaped, she didn't bring up his suggestion that they would return to France one day. There were moments when she'd caught a distant, almost haunted look darkening his eyes. At those times she guessed his mind was back at the Chapelle, wondering how little Remy was doing, as she often thought about Clairdy. She wanted to talk about it but his demeanor at these quiet times told her not to. He might not admit it but he felt guilty about leaving that boy. She understood his reasons. She wondered some times if Mateo did.

What she owed for her return airfare had been paid back and to set all the records straight she spoke to Mama on the phone, admitting that she'd taken her money under false pretenses, that she'd never planned to return to Italy. To Bailey's surprise, Mama had said she'd guessed as much and understood. She might be a dear friend of Emilio's grandmother, but she had never been a big fan of that boy... not since Emilio had tried to fight her Mateo so many years earlier.

Mama had gone on to say that when his ring had returned in the mail, Emilio had spread word that his Australian fiancée had indeed run out on him. But he hadn't pined for long. Emilio was seeing another lady, this one a visitor from Wales. Mama said she was a nice young woman and she would keep an eye out for her too.

Now that her more recent past issues were ironed out, Bailey felt a need to at least try to make some kind of amends with her father. They hadn't spoken in over a year and she'd grown a great deal since then. Perhaps it was foolish hoping but maybe he'd grown too. Whereas a couple of weeks ago, when she'd seen him on the street, she hadn't known if she were strong enough, now, this morning, in her heart she believed she could not only face her father, but if their meeting turned sour—if he still shunned and criticized her—she could do what was needed to go forward with her life.

She could forgive him and walk away.

Now the inquiring smile in Mateo's eyes dimmed and he scraped his chair to turn more toward her. "You want to go see your father now? This morning?"

When she nodded, he ran a hand through his hair, smiled and pushed his chair back. "In that case I'll get the car out."

He got to his feet but, before he could head off, she caught his arm.

"Mateo, you don't have to come."

His dark brows knitted. "Do you want me there?"

A spool of recent memories unwound…how Mateo had helped her with the money she'd owed Mama. How he'd given her a roof over her head, even when she'd insisted she didn't need one. The way he'd invited her into his life, through friends like Alex and Natalie and Nichole. The amazing time he'd shown her in France.

He'd trusted her enough to admit that he would give anything to ask his own father *why*. She'd realized that was precisely what she needed to ask too.

Decided, she pushed to her feet. "If you'd like to come, that would mean a lot."

As they pulled up outside the familiar Sydney address, Bailey dug her toes into her shoes and told herself to get a grip. She wasn't a kid anymore. She was here not because she needed her father but because she *chose* to see him. If he turned her away…well, she'd deal with it. She'd been through worse. And with Mateo standing alongside of her, she could face anything.

Mateo's strong, warm hand folded around hers.

"You'll be fine."

She tilted her head at the front yard. A good part of the greenery lay hidden behind a massive brick and iron fence.

"I grew up playing on that lawn," she said. "The summer after I got a bike for Christmas, my father built a track on the other side of that garage, complete with dirt jumps and dips. He said he'd take me to moto-X competitions, if I wanted."

"Not your thing?"

"I turned seven that year and discovered my destiny. I was going to be either a Labradoodle breeder or a Russian circus fairy."

His eyes crinkled at the corners at the same time his mouth slanted and some of the stress grabbing between her shoulder blades eased.

"I ditched after-school circus skills mid-third term," she explained. "I still love poodle crosses though. Dad said he'd set me up with my own breeder's kennel when I was older."

Mateo curled a loose strand of hair behind her ear. "Everything will be fine."

"Promise?"

"I promise you won't regret coming here today," he said, then pushed open his door.

Together they walked up the path to the front door. Mateo stood back while she flexed her hands a few times then rang the bell. Her heartbeat galloping, she waited an interminable time, but the hardwood door she knew so well failed to open.

Feeling beads of perspiration break on her brow, she glanced across. Mateo cocked his chin at the door and, with a shaky hand, she thumbed the bell again. After several more nothing-happening moments, she surrendered and threw up her hands.

"All that build-up and he's out."

She pivoted on her heel, ready to leave, but Mateo only stood firm.

"It's Sunday morning," he said, running a reassuring palm down her arm. "Give him a chance to put down the paper. Set his coffee cup on the sink."

Listening to a kookaburra laugh from a nearby treetop, Bailey gathered her failing courage and faced that closed door again. A neighbor, trimming hedges, popped his head over the fence. Smiling, Mateo nodded at the curious gray-haired man. But Bailey only blew out a done-with-it sigh.

"If my father's in there, he's not coming out."

After a few seconds, Mateo reluctantly agreed. They'd turned to leave when that heavy door cracked open. A man in a weekend checked shirt squinted at them through a shaft of steamy morning light. While Bailey's chest tightened, Damon Ross's eyes flared and his grasp on the doorjamb firmed as if his knees had given way.

"Bailey...?" His head angled as he took in more of her. "It is you, isn't it?"

She tried to swallow but her throat was suddenly desert dry. So, although it wobbled at the corners, she tried a smile instead.

"How are you, Dad?"

Stepping back, her father ran his gaze up and down again as if she might be an apparition come back to haunt him. But then his expression softened and the stern voice she'd come to know over these last years softened too. He even partway smiled when he said, "I wasn't sure I'd ever see you again."

She shrugged. "I didn't know if you wanted to see me."

Her father moved forward, hesitated, and then reached his arms out. Bringing her in, he hugged his only daughter close and for a bittersweet moment she was transported back to that day when they'd desperately needed each other. The day her mother had been laid to rest.

Bailey gave herself over to the feeling. This is how she'd dreamed this meeting would unwind. The smell of his aftershave, the warmth of his bristled cheek pressed to hers. As tears stung behind her eyes, she wanted to say how much she missed him but as he released her and edged back, she gathered herself. Hopefully, there would be plenty of time for that.

Damon Ross acknowledged the third person standing nearby. The older man drew back his shoulders and extended his hand.

"We haven't met."

Mateo, several inches taller, took her father's hand. "Mateo Celeca."

"Have you known my daughter long?"

"Only a few weeks."

Her father's calculating lawyer's gaze took Mateo in before, obviously approving, he released another smile and waved them both inside.

"Are you from Sydney, Mateo?" Her father asked, escorting them through the foyer that wasn't a quarter as large as Mateo's.

"Originally from Italy."

"The name, the complexion…" Damon Ross lobbed a knowing look over his shoulder. "I guessed Mediterranean."

The aroma of coffee brewing led them to the kitchen. While the men made small talk, Bailey discovered the cups in the same cupboard and poured three coffees before they sat down in the adjoining meals area.

The table was stacked with journals and assorted papers relating to her father's work. The rest of the room looked clean. Almost too tidy. Didn't seem so long ago that her mother's easel and paints had occupied that far corner, the one that offered the best natural light. Ann Ross had always kept a spare pair of slippers right there by the door. Of course, they were gone now. But her parents' wedding portrait still hung in the center of that feature wall. Sipping coffee, Bailey wondered whether their bedroom had changed. Whether her mother's clothes were still hanging in the wardrobe all these years later.

"You had a good time overseas?" Her father's dark-winged eyebrows arched as he lifted the cup to his pursed lips.

"Yes." Bailey fought the urge to clear her throat. "Thank you. I did."

"I'm glad." Her father held his smile. "You must have been busy."

A little nervous, she laughed. "Pretty much."

"You enjoyed it then?" Damon Ross went on.

Her fingers tightened around the cup. He was pushing the point that he had advised her not to go abroad alone. Digging to see if, true to his prediction, anything had gone wrong.

"I'm glad I went," she said, her smile verging on tight now. "I'm glad I'm back."

Her father nodded, but his buoyant expression had slipped a touch, too.

"I wasn't sure what to think," he said.

Out of the corner of her eye, Bailey saw Mateo roll back one shoulder a second before she replied. "About what?"

"About how you were doing," her father expounded as if he were telling her B followed A. "Whether you were in any kind of trouble."

"You didn't need to worry, Dad."

Damon Ross laughed with little humor. "It's not as if I've never had to worry before."

A retort, fast and hot, leapt up her throat but before she

could say a word, her father changed his tone…upbeat again.

"So," he pushed his cup aside and threaded his fingers on the table, "did you find work while you were over there?"

"I did some waitressing."

"Well, as long as it kept you out of trouble."

Bailey's face burned. There was that word again. Or was he merely being inquiring, genuinely concerned, and she was being overly sensitive? Now that she was here, shouldn't she be the better person and let any slights, intended or otherwise, sail over her head? She was mature enough to handle this.

"How did you two meet?" her father asked Mateo while Bailey took a long sip of hot coffee.

Mateo replied, "Through a mutual friend."

"Bailey's mother and I met at a church function." Damon blinked several times then dropped his faraway gaze. "But that was a long time ago."

"We recently returned from France," Mateo chipped in, sharing a covert you'll-be-fine wink with her.

Her father's wistful smiled returned. "My wife and I visited Paris on our honeymoon. Ann was taken with the country scenery. She said she felt as if she'd stepped into a Monet." His gaze wandered to his daughter and he sat back. "So, what are you doing with yourself nowadays?"

"I'm working," she announced. "For a real estate firm."

Mateo stepped in again. "Bailey and a friend of mine clicked. Natalie said Bailey had what her agency was looking for." He caught her gaze. "Didn't she, darling?"

Bailey's heart lifted to her throat. Mateo had only ever addressed her by name and yet he'd chosen this moment to call her an endearment. A well-educated, respected professional in his field, Damon Ross was challenging his daughter and Mateo was defending her without causing waves, by letting her father know she was his "darling" and insinuating she was selling properties rather than cleaning bathrooms.

She hoped the smile in her eyes told Mateo she appreciated his efforts. But honestly, she'd sooner he didn't intervene. Whatever came today, she needed to stand up for herself, not as a child standing toe to toe with a disapproving parent, but as the self-respecting adult she'd become, and without too much of her father's help.

"Bailey's going back to school," Mateo was saying.

Her father looked half impressed. "Well, well. I said one day you'd regret dropping out." While Bailey set her teeth, Damon Ross spoke again to Mateo. "My daughter didn't attain her high school diploma," he said under his breath as if she hadn't learned to spell her own name.

Bailey studied that wedding portrait and, hands on the table's edge, pushed her chair out. She'd come here hoping—she'd wanted to make their father-daughter relationship work—but she was only hurting herself. Still, she wouldn't argue. Neither would she sit here a moment longer.

As she rose, her father stopped talking and looked up at her with eyes that, for a moment, were unguarded.

"Are you pouring more coffee?" he asked.

"Actually, Dad, we have to go."

Her father got to his feet. "You only just arrived."

"We can stay awhile longer," Mateo said, standing too.

But she pinned Mateo with a firm look that said he was wrong.

"Mateo," she said, "it's time to go."

While her father muttered that he didn't know what the rush was all about, Mateo's furrowed gaze questioned hers.

She peered up at the ceiling and almost groaned. She appreciated Mateo coming—appreciated everything he'd done—but this was her business. *Her* life. She'd gone through this game with her father too many times already.

Bailey walked away and the men's footfalls followed. At the door, she leaned toward her father and pressed a quick kiss to his cheek. When she drew back, her father's gaze was lowered on her wrist. On the bracelet.

"I see you haven't lost it yet," he said.

Her gaze went from the bracelet to her father's cheated look and a suffocating surge of hurt, and guilt, bubbled up inside her.

He just couldn't let her leave without mentioning that.

On the edge, she flicked open the bracelet's new clasp. "Know what, Dad?" Slipping the chain and its jingling charms from her wrist, she handed it over. "I want you to have this."

His brow furrowed. "But I gave it to *you*."

"Not the way I needed. The way she would've wanted you to."

"Don't start on—"

"Mum didn't ask to die," she plowed on. "She didn't want to leave us. I don't need this to know she loved me. It's sad but," she slapped the bracelet in his palm, "I think you need this more than me."

She headed down the path.

Mateo remote-unlocked his car a second before she reached for the passenger side handle. Churning inside, she kept her burning, disappointed gaze dead ahead while Mateo slid into the driver's side. He belted up, ignited the engine, shifted the gear into drive. Trying to even her breathing, she felt his gaze slide over.

"Your father's waiting on the doorstep," he told her. "Don't you think you ought to at least wave?"

Her stomach kicked and she screwed her eyes shut. "Don't try to make me feel guiltier than I already do."

Not about her father's behavior but because she *had* almost lost that bracelet, and she would never have forgiven herself if she had.

Mateo wrung the steering wheel with both hands. "He was a little out of line. But, Bailey, he's your father. We were there ten minutes. Do you really want to walk away, cut him off, again?"

Eyes burning, she continued to stare ahead. Mateo might want the chance to sit down and speak with his biological father, but she knew now hers would never listen. Would never understand. He wasn't the only one who'd felt lost when Ann Ross had died.

And while they were on the subject—if she was running away, hadn't Mateo in a sense run away too, from that little boy who would love to be his son?

But she wouldn't mention that. If she did, they'd have an argument and the way she was feeling—the way she'd thatched her fingers to stop her hands from shaking—she wouldn't be the one to back down.

While she glared out the windshield, Mateo sucked in an audible breath and wrenched the car away from the curb. They drove in silence home. When she got out of the car, she tried to make her way through the house and up that staircase before any tears could fall, but Mateo had other plans. Catching up, he grabbed her arm from behind. Tamping down hot emotion, she lifted her chin and turned around.

The chiseled plains of his face were set. "We need to talk."

"Not now."

She tried to wind away but he held her firm. "Don't let this get to you."

"I'd have thought you'd approve of me walking away."

Mateo had once said he was selfish. He was wrong. He was a hypocrite. Mateo might have had a good relationship with Ernesto, but there was a little boy back in France who had silently begged for years for the monsieur to accept him. Not so different from the way she wanted to be accepted by her father.

She shook her arm free and started up the stairs. It was better they didn't discuss it.

Mateo's steps sounded behind her. "I'm not the one you're angry with."

Her throat aching, she ground out, "Please. Mateo." *Please.* She continued up the stairs. "Leave me alone."

When an arm lassoed her waist and pitched her around, she let out a gasp as she fell. But before her back met the uneven ramp of the stairs, that arm was there again, scooped under and supporting her as Mateo hovered over her, daring her to try to walk away from him again.

But he didn't speak, and the longer he stayed leaning over her as she lay on the steps, his eyes searching hers, the more her tide of anger ebbed and gradually seeped away. But the hurt remained...for herself as well as for Remy. She doubted that would ever leave.

Her words came out a hoarse whisper.

"Why does he do that?"

Mateo exhaled and stroked her hair. "I don't know."

"I won't ever go back."

"You don't have to...if that's what you want."

Frustration sparked again. "I know what I want, Mateo."

His lips brushed her brow. "I know what *I* want."

She shifted onto her elbows. "Do you?"

He hesitated a heartbeat before his mouth slanted over and took hers.

His kiss was tender and at the same time passionate. Dissolving into the emotion, needing to completely melt away and forget, she reached for his chest and struggled with his shirt buttons. As the kiss deepened, he shifted too, rolling back each shoulder in turn as she peeled the sleeves off his powerful arms.

When his mouth finally left hers, her blood felt on fire. She didn't want to think about anything but this. Not her father or France or her bracelet. Only how Mateo made her feel time and again. She couldn't deny it any longer. As much as she'd set out to keep her head and her heart, she'd fallen in love with Mateo, an emotion that consumed her more and more each day.

His eyes closed, one arm curled around her head, he murmured against her parted lips. "Perhaps we ought to take this upstairs."

She sighed against his cheek. "If you want."

His brow pinched. Before he kissed her again, he said, "I want you."

Fifteen

Finished tapping in the final answer on the last form, Bailey held her breath and hit send. If everything went according to plan, in a couple of months she'd be busy studying, sending off her first assignments, on her way to getting that degree.

Sitting back in Mateo's home office chair, she had to grin over the majors she'd chosen. What were the odds? Then again, what were the odds she'd come to feel this way, this *deeply,* about Mateo?

A week had passed since their surprise visit to her father's house…since Mateo had defended her, challenged her, then pinned her on the stairs where they'd made love in a frenzied, soul stirring way they never had before. Her skin flashed hot to even think of the avalanche of emotions he'd brought out in her that day.

Mateo cared about her. He enjoyed her company. But even more, Mateo Celeca *believed* in her. Yes, for her sake he hoped she and her father could somehow, someday, make amends, but he respected her enough not to push. The same way she wouldn't push about Remy, no matter how strongly she felt those two should be together.

More and more she was coming to believe she and Mateo should stay together too. More than common sense said he could have his choice of companions, and yet he chose to be with her. Had asked her to stay. She couldn't help but wonder....

Exhaling, Bailey pushed that thought aside and, before signing off the computer, decided to check emails. A message from her friend Vicky Jackson popped up in reply to the email Bailey had sent when she'd discovered that first day back that her friend was out of town. Vicky was dying to hear all the news. Had she seen her dad yet? Had she met anyone wonderful? As always, Vicky wanted the gossip, just like the old days, bolts and all.

Bailey glanced around Mateo's red leather and rosewood office. So many amazing collectors' items. Even the ornate silver letter opener looked as if it belonged in a museum. Would her friend since school believe what had happened over the last few months? From backpacking around Europe, to settling down in Casa Buona, to being cornered into an engagement that had sent her on a desperate flight home to Australia. Best of all she'd gone and lost her heart. A huge romantic, when Vicky found out, she would go berserk!

Fingers on keys, she jumped right in.

Vicky! You wouldn't believe how I've lucked out. So much has happened since we saw each other last. But the main thing is that I found *the* guy. A keeper!

I'm sitting here now in his home study. Make that mansion! I'm actually cleaning houses atm. Long story.

But that's only temporary. I have *so* many plans—BIG plans—and Doctor Mateo Celeca is at the center of them all—

Bailey stopped, pricked her ears and listened. Mateo's car was cruising up the drive.

She tapped out a super quick "Talk soon," hit send, then jumped up. Mateo had said she could use this laptop anytime. She didn't feel guilty about taking him at his word. In fact, she'd come to feel wonderfully at home here. But, with him being gone for four hours, she was excited to have him back. Whenever she thought of him striding toward her, that dazzling smile reaching out and warming her all over, her knees went weak. She needed his kiss. More and more she wanted so much to let him know how deeply she felt.

What would he say if she did?

Mateo entered the house aware of the weight in his shirt pocket and the broad grin on his face.

Not so long ago he'd had no intention of getting overly involved with a woman. And yet, with Bailey, he was involved up to his chin. He'd spent his whole life avoiding the ghosts and hurdles of his past. He'd only needed his friends and the possessions he surrounded himself with. To open his heart—to consider marriage and children of his own—would mean to invite in vulnerability. Take on risk.

But late last night in the shadows, after he and Bailey had made love and he'd felt so at peace, he'd questioned himself. Searched his soul.

Did he *love* Bailey Ross?

Moving down the central hall now, Mateo rolled the question over in his mind but still the answer eluded him. He did know, however, that he had never felt this attracted to a woman before. He enjoyed, without reservation, Bailey's conversations and smiles. He looked forward to seeing her, kissing her, letting her know how much he valued her. And they were certainly beyond compatible in the bedroom.

In Paris he'd made a decision. To offer her commitment—a home, his affection—without unnecessary encumbrances. This morning he'd come to a different conclusion.

He may not be certain that he loved Bailey but he was wise enough to know he would never find this connection with anyone else. Today he intended to utter words that previously had not existed in his personal vocabulary. As soon as he found her, wherever she was hiding, he intended to ask her to be his bride.

He entered the kitchen, swung a glance around. Empty. Out in "their" garden, no sign of her among the statues either. A hand cupped around his mouth, he called out, "Bailey. I'm back."

He waited but the house was quiet. Then he had a thought. Before he'd left this morning, she'd asked if she could use his computer. A bounce in his step, he headed for the office.

A few seconds later he discovered that room empty too. But from the doorway he saw the internet browser on his laptop had been left open. The world was full of hackers, scammers, looking for a window to wiggle into and defraud. A person couldn't be too careful. Needing to log off, he crossed over and saw a message hadn't been closed. He moved the curser to save the draft at the same time a few words caught his eye.

BIG plans... A keeper...

His gaze slid to the top of the screen. He skimmed the entire message, lowered into his chair and read it again. After a fourth time, Mateo's hand bunched into a tight ball on the desk. There had to be a different way to interpret it. A different light from the murky one he'd latched on to. But, for the life of him, he couldn't grasp any other implication from this message than the one hitting him square between the eyes.

You wouldn't believe how I've lucked out. I found...a keeper!

Actually cleaning houses...that's only temporary... BIG plans—and Doctor Mateo Celeca is at the center of them all—

His gut kicked then twisted into a dozen sickening knots while his hand drifted to his shirt pocket. His fingers curled over the velvet pouch inside and tightened. Was her meaning as obvious as it seemed? Had he been wrong about Bailey? Emilio then Mama...Had she wormed her way into his feelings to manipulate him too?

Had he played the fool *again?*

"Mateo!" Bailey's call came from down the hall. "Where are you?"

He snapped back to the here and now and dabbed his clammy brow with his forearm. He had to think.

"Mateo?"

The call sounded close. He looked over and saw Bailey standing at the office door, looking slightly flushed, a brilliant smile painted across her face. She rushed forward and wasted no time plopping onto his lap and snatching a quick kiss.

"Guess what I did today?" She asked, beaming.

Although his mind was steaming, he kept his tone level. "Why don't you tell me?"

"I enrolled."

He forced a smile. "You did?"

"After looking into all the faculties' courses and searching myself about what I really wanted to accomplish, you won't believe what I've decided to be."

Out the corner of his eye, that email seemed to taunt him. "What did you decide?"

"I want to study law. Not criminal, like Dad, but human rights. I want to do my best helping those who don't have the education or means or, in some cases, the status to help themselves."

"That sounds…worthy."

Absently watching the motion, she curled some hair behind his ear. Where normally he would lean in against her touch, this minute it was all he could do not to wince. She had big plans.

Who was this woman?

Did he know her at all?

"Bridging courses are the first step," she went on, "a chance to catch up on high school stuff before tackling the full on units." She let out a happy sigh. "I'm so excited." Nuzzling down into his neck, she murmured against his jaw. "I missed you today. Where have you been?"

Mateo thought of the item in his pocket, and the rock that filled the space where his heart used to beat grew harder still. He shut his eyes and groaned. God, he wished he'd never seen that note.

Her cuddling stopped. Her lashes fluttered against his neck an instant before she drew away and searched his eyes, head slanting as she reached to cup his cheek.

"Is something wrong?"

His gaze penetrated hers as his jaw clenched more. He should ask her point blank, lay it on the table, and this time he wouldn't be hoodwinked. How could he be when the truth was there on that screen in black and white?

"You left your inbox open," he ground out.

She bit her lip. "Sorry. I rushed off when I heard your car."

"You sent a message to a friend."

She blinked. "That's right."

"It didn't go through."

Her brow furrowed and her gaze shot to the screen before it slid back to him. He could sense her mind ticking over. "Did you read it?"

When he moved, she shifted and he got to his feet.

"Mateo…"

He headed for the door. His throat wouldn't stop convulsing. He needed fresh air. Needed to get out of here and be alone for a while. But she stayed on his heels.

"Mateo, tell me what's wrong."

He peered down toward the foyer, to his elaborate staircase that, as large and grand as it was, didn't really lead anywhere…except to more furniture and art and antiques. He'd accumulated so much. Right now he felt as if he'd been stripped of everything.

When she touched his arm, his stomach jumped. He tried to find his calm center as he edged around. Her beautiful pale blue eyes were clouded with uncertainty, the indigo band around each iris darker than he'd ever seen. Blood pounded and crashed in his ears. She'd been caught and she knew it.

The words—his accusation—were on the tip of his tongue when the doorbell sounded. He thought of ignoring it, but he couldn't get what he needed to off his chest with some unknown person lurking on his doorstep. Leaving a desolate Bailey, he strode over, opened the door and was caught between a groan and smile.

Alex Ramirez stood with his hands in his pockets. Natalie, looking as beautiful as ever, was at her husband's side. Reece sat perched on her hip.

"We were on our way to a picnic," Alex said, sliding his

shades back on his head. "We thought you guys might want to join us."

"It's such a gorgeous day," Natalie added breezily, but a certain shadow in her eyes let him know something was amiss. Perhaps she was just overly tired.

"A picnic?" Bailey came forward. "I'd love to get out," she said as she looked across, "but Mateo might have something planned."

Mateo stepped aside. "Come in out of the heat."

"We have plenty of food and drink." Natalie entered the foyer while Reece kicked his legs as if he was riding a horse. "There's chicken and homemade potato salad. And plenty of room in the car. When you start a family you need to trade sports cars for roomier, safer options."

Mateo didn't miss the emphasis Natalie placed on *safer* or the way Alex's lips pressed together as he looked down and crossed his arms.

Mateo folded his arms too as he shared a look between them. "Is something wrong?"

Alex said, "No," at the same time Natalie said, "Actually, we wanted to speak with you—"

Alex groaned out a cautionary, *"Nat."*

"—about France," she finished.

And something else. Something important enough for them to show up unannounced. Not that he minded friends dropping in, but beneath the cheery exterior, some kind of trouble was upsetting Nat and Alex's usual state of marital bliss. And it seemed Natalie, at least, wanted him to referee.

Unfortunately, this was far from the ideal time. But he couldn't simply turn his good friends around and on their way. Not when Natalie's eyes were pleading with him to leave with them.

Mateo unfolded his arms. "Sure," he said, smiling, "we'd love to go."

Bailey spun on her heel. "Let me just race upstairs for a moment."

Natalie headed down the hall. "Do you mind if I use a bathroom? Reece sicked up a little on his shirt. He's had a cough."

"Of course." Mateo ran an assessing eye over the baby, but he didn't look flushed or ill. A little restless perhaps. "You know where the closest one is."

Alex waited until Natalie was out of earshot before he stepped closer.

"Sorry about this."

"No need to apologize. You're welcome any time."

There were simply more convenient times than others.

"It was Nat's idea we drop in. She values your opinion." Alex shrugged. "I do too."

"What's the problem?"

"Nat wanted to pin you down to get your take on—"

"All set!"

Alex stopped mid-sentence and both men's attention swung to the stairs. Bailey was bouncing down, a big bag over her shoulder. When she reached the foyer floor, she glanced around. "Where's Nat?"

"Here we are."

Natalie emerged, baby Reece resting on her hip, his cheek on her shoulder. Carefully, she handed him over to Alex. "I'm afraid he's getting a little too heavy for Mummy to carry."

"Babies do grow up," Alex said, swinging Reece onto his own hip.

"But they still need protecting."

"In lots of ways," Alex pointed out.

Mateo opened the door. "We should go."

As they headed out the door, Bailey went to loop her arm through his but he hadn't forgotten that email. How the truth had made him feel. Grinding his back teeth, he hastened his step, caught up with Alex and helped him put Reece in his seat.

As they all buckled up and Alex pulled out down the drive, Bailey tried to keep her spirits high even though she felt completely off balance.

When Mateo had come home she'd been on cloud nine. Now, for reasons she couldn't explain, there was nothing but tension all around. Between Mateo and her. Alex and Natalie. Even Mateo and Alex! Hugging the gift bag containing that builder's kit close, she studied Reece when he coughed. Even the baby didn't seem overly happy.

As if to prove it, the little guy barked again.

Natalie swung around to check on him but Alex put his hand on her arm and spoke to those in the back, as if he wanted to divert the focus.

"So tell me, has Paris changed?"

Mateo was glaring out the window. "The Louvre's still there."

"So you said hello to the *Mona Lisa?*"

Bailey answered Alex this time. "It was amazing to see her for real."

"And the orphanage?"

Mateo again. "Going well."

"Did you see that little boy? Remy?" Natalie peered around again. "Is he still there?"

"Quite a few have found families," Mateo said, and Bailey almost shivered at his tone. A stay-away-from-that-subject-today timbre.

Still, Natalie persisted. "But not Remy? He hasn't found a home yet?"

When Mateo's hands bunched on his lap, Bailey answered for him.

"Remy's still there. Barely says a word. But his little girlfriend makes up for it. Clairdy never stops talking."

"How old is he now?" Natalie persisted. "Five? Six?"

Mateo leaned forward. "This is a good park. Plenty of shade. Great views of the harbor."

Alex pulled in and they unloaded the picnic basket from the back while Natalie and Bailey took care of the baby. They found a shady spot overlooking the blue water and spread out two large checkered blankets.

"Would you like to go again?" Natalie placed Reece down and fished for a toy to occupy him from her diaper bag. "To France, I mean?"

"Actually, we'd kind of discussed that." Bailey slid a glance over.

Mateo's chest tightened as he took in her curious look. "Depends on my schedule," he replied as he found the thermos.

Bailey could go to France again but it wouldn't be with him. She'd exchanged paying back the price of her ticket home from Italy for an all-expenses first-class trip to Europe. She'd done well. And when they were alone again, he'd tell her exactly that—a moment before he told her to pack her bag and leave.

He'd had doubts from the start. And when that security guard had delayed them in Paris, he'd suffered more than a niggle. Now he knew why. There was reason to be suspicious. Hell, even her own father didn't trust her.

"Which part did you like best?" Natalie was saying, handing Reece a clear ball with jigsaw cut-outs and corresponding shapes inside.

"There were so many amazing things." Bailey fumbled as she laid out the plastic plates and they went in all directions over the blanket. "I couldn't choose just one."

Reece threw the ball then let out another cough and another. Mateo's doctor antennae went up.

"Has he had that long?"

"A couple of days," Natalie said.

Alex added, "But the doctor explained he couldn't give him his scheduled shots until he's completely well."

"*If* we decide he should be immunized," Natalie said.

Alex ran a hand through his hair. "Nat, we've discussed this."

"No. *You* made a decision for all three of us."

Reece began to grumble. Making *shushing* sounds, Natalie folded down beside him and handed back the ball.

Alex set his hands on his hips. "Mateo, save me. Tell her children need to be immunized."

"But there are side effects," Natalie interjected. "Sometimes serious ones. There are risks, aren't there, Mateo?"

Mateo considered the two of them—Natalie so passionate about protecting her boy from possible harm, Alex in exactly the same position, just looking at possible dangers differently. No one ever said parenting was easy. This decision might be a no-brainer for a lot of folks. For others, whether or not to immunize was the beginning of a whole host of moral battles associated with the responsibilities of being a mother or father. He should thank Bailey for inadvertently showing him her true colors and saving him from all this.

"In my professional opinion," he began, "I would have to say that the benefits far outweigh any possible dangers."

Natalie's slim nostrils flared then she dropped her gaze. "It's not that easy when it's your own child, Mateo." Holding her brow, she pushed out a breath and apologized. "I'm sorry. There was just this horrible story on the news the other night about the possible effects of shots. The footage was shocking. And then Sally from work said she knew of a couple who had a similar experience with their toddler. He was never the same again." Natalie peered up with haunted eyes. "Some kids *die*. Once it's done you can't take it back."

Mateo scrubbed his jaw. Natalie did need sleep. And reassurance. This decision obviously meant a lot to her. To both of them. As it should. But it wasn't *his* decision.

When Reece began to whimper, confused at seeing his mother upset, Alex crossed over, kneeled beside his family and hugged them tight. He brushed the words over his wife's crown. "We'll work it out, darling. Don't worry."

Mateo sat down with his friends and while Bailey made chicken sandwiches, he spoke to Natalie and Alex candidly. With any vaccination there could be side effects, but most often minor ones. Immunization was a way to curb and even eliminate deadly diseases in both children and adults. Ultimately the burden of research and decision was on the parents' shoulders.

But he conceded…Natalie was right. Rationalizing must sound pat when the child concerned wasn't your own. Natalie seemed reassured somewhat.

In the dappled sunshine, they finished their sandwiches—Reece ate almost a whole one. The packing up had begun when Bailey remembered. "I left something in the car."

She returned with a gift bag and handed it to Natalie. "This is for Reece. Mateo picked it out."

Mateo averted his gaze. He'd been happy to choose the gift but memories of the day also brought back the image of that security guard and his own suspicions. Come to think of it, Bailey hadn't emptied her pockets that day. She'd merely pulled out the bracelet.

But that was all water under the bridge. As charming as she was, that email had proven her more mercenary nature beyond a doubt. Duped by her own hand. He didn't care what excuses she came up with.

Natalie helped Reece unwrap the gift. He instantly grabbed

the hammer and thumped the ground. He squealed with delight when the tool squeaked and whistled.

Alex gently ruffled his son's head. "That's my boy."

Mateo took in the scene and knew he ought to be happy for them. But, even when he wanted to deny them, the truth was that other emotions were winning out. Ugly emotions like envy and disappointment.

This morning he'd come home thinking that soon he would be a married man. He'd been prepared to do what three months ago no one could have convinced him to try. He'd wanted to risk. Was willing to try for a family of his own. After finding the truth out about Bailey, he would never consider taking that kind of risk again.

After they'd packed up, Alex and Natalie dropped them home. Mateo headed for the door without waiting. He knew Bailey would follow, and out of the earshot of neighbors, he'd tell her precisely what he thought.

Bailey stood, stunned, watching Mateo's broad shoulders roll away as he ascended the stairs to his porch then unlocked and entered the house. She held her sick stomach, unable to comprehend how he could be so angry over that email to Vicky. Yes, she'd been pretty open in suggesting she thought there was—and wanted there to be—a future for them. She knew how he felt about marriage and children. God knows she hadn't wanted to get this involved either.

But now he was acting as though she was some weirdo with an attachment disorder. After the way he'd treated her—like a princess—*dammit,* that just wasn't fair. He'd led her on, set her up to trust him and...yes, *love* him. She thought he was falling in love with her too.

Back straight, she started for the stairs.

If he thought she would cower in a corner and accept this

behavior—the way Mateo had intimated she ought to take her father's sorry treatment—he was sadly mistaken.

When she strode in the door, he was waiting for her by the stairs. Given her dark expression, he knew what to expect. She was primed to defend herself, but he wasn't prepared to let this demise ramble on. He'd get to the point. Then she could leave.

"These past years I thought I had everything I could ever want," he told her as she crossed over to where he stood. "I thought I was content. And then I met you."

A range of emotions flashed over her face. First happiness. Lastly suspicion. "I'm not sure what you're saying."

"When I came home earlier I intended to ask you to marry me."

He extracted the blue jewelry pouch from his shirt pocket, loosened the string and tipped the ring into his palm. Five carats. The jeweler said his fiancée would love it. More than ever, Mateo felt certain that she would have.

Her incredulous gaze drifted from the ring to his eyes. Then her cheeks pinked up and her throat made a muted high-pitched noise.

"When you were out this morning you bought this?"

He inspected the diamond, tipping the stone so the light caught then radiated pale geometric patterns on the walls.

"I wasn't sure of the fit," he said. "The jeweler said I could take it back." That was precisely what he intended to do now. His fingers closed over the stone and his voice lowered to a rough-edged growl. "You have no idea how betrayed I felt when I read that email."

Bailey simply stared, looking as if she were taken aback and even annoyed. "Betrayed is a pretty strong word."

He almost sneered. "I shouldn't feel manipulated when you told that friend you wouldn't be cleaning floors for long?"

"I said that because eventually I'll get my degree."

"What you said was that you had big plans. That you'd lucked out."

"Well, I did feel lucky to have—" she stopped, blinked, then coughed out a humorless laugh.

"Wait a minute. You think I'm here...that I share your bed..." Her eyes glistened at the same time her face pinched as if she'd swallowed a teaspoon of salt. "You think I'm sleeping with you for your *money?*"

He huffed. "I'm sure as hell not sleeping with you because of yours."

When her eyes filled with moisture and hurt, Mateo cursed as a blade sliced between his ribs and twisted.

He inhaled deeply. "I apologize. I shouldn't have said that."

"Mateo, if you felt you needed to say it, believe me, I needed to hear it."

She wound around him and started up the stairs.

He called after her. "So you're going."

She stopped at the same spot where they'd made love a few days before. Her face was pale. Her hands trembled, even as they gripped the banister. He imagined she felt determined... and maybe, with her plans ruined, even crushed.

Join the club.

"You truly believe I'm nothing but a gold digger?"

He should have been prepared for it. The threat of tears. The indignation. Of course she wasn't going to admit it. "Bailey, there's no other way to read it."

Through narrowed eyes, she nodded as if she were seeing him for the first time.

"I'm such a fool."

"And how does that feel?"

She ignored his sarcasm. "Could you believe I thought you

were upset because you'd found out I'd fallen in love with you?"

His head kicked back but then that certain coldness rose up again. "Don't play with me."

"This morning I thought I'd really found the perfect guy, that fate had finally smiled on me again. An intelligent, good-looking professional with a sense of humor who had a heart to boot. Hell, I thought you were way too good for me." She dropped over her shoulder as she continued up the stairs, "Turns out I'm too good for you."

Sixteen

Bailey had been packed and gone from Mateo Celeca's house in ten minutes flat. He wasn't anywhere around, and she was glad of it. Nothing he could say would change her mind about leaving, and if she'd seen his supercilious face, she would have needed to let him know again how disappointed she was. Disappointed in herself as well. For believing and hoping too much.

Now, a week later she was entering Natalie's real estate office. The receptionist buzzed through and a moment later Natalie breezed out from a back office, the smile wide on her face. She beckoned Bailey inside.

"I wasn't expecting you."

"I just finished cleaning my last house for the day. I hope this isn't an inconvenient time." Bailey took a seat while Natalie shut her office door then lowered into a chair behind her orderly desk.

"What can I do for you? Personal or private?"

"Both. You obviously don't know yet. Mateo and I broke up last week."

Her expression dropped. "I can't believe it. You said you'd had such a perfect time in France."

"We did. So perfect I fell in love with him."

Natalie nodded as if she understood. "He hasn't tried to contact you since you left?"

"No. And I don't want him to."

"He's always said he didn't want to know about vows and rings." Annoyed, Natalie flicked a pencil away. "I love Mateo but he's so stubborn on that. People come into our lives. Things change."

"Actually, Mateo bought a ring. The most beautiful ring I've ever seen."

Natalie's eyes rounded. "He proposed and you said no?"

Bailey relayed the story about the email, how Mateo had misinterpreted the message and how he wasn't prepared to view it from a different, more flattering light.

"I'm sorry," Natalie said, "but it sounds like a timely excuse to me." Bailey waited for her to explain. "For Mateo to have gone so far as to buy a diamond, he *must* be in love with you. But it doesn't sound as if he's ready to look beyond the past."

"I know he has issues with family. That he feels as if his parents abandoned him, his biological father particularly."

That was a big part of the reason he kept his emotions concerning Remy reined in so tight.

"There's something else," Natalie admitted. "Mateo was in love once before, many years ago. From what Alex tells me, she was not a nice type. She preyed on Mateo's good nature and generosity. He gave and gave but nothing was ever enough. They'd have arguments then make up. Alex said Mateo wasn't prepared to ever go through that kind of rollercoaster affair again. It scared him to think what would happen if he married a self-centered woman like that and they had a family. If he died and she abandoned the children."

Bailey tried to absorb the details as she gazed blindly at some document on the desk. "He wanted to marry her and she used him…."

"She didn't so much use him as bleed him dry."

Bailey's gaze flew up. "I wasn't with Mateo because of his money, what he could give me—"

"Oh, honey, I know."

Natalie skirted the desk and put her arms around her, but that didn't help Bailey from feeling gutted. She understood his reasoning a little better, but whatever lay in his past, Mateo was wrong to have jumped to any conclusions without giving her an opportunity to explain. She was tired of feeling as if she weren't good enough. As if she continually had to prove herself.

Moving away, Natalie leaned back on the edge of the desk. "Would you like Alex to talk to him?"

Bailey shook her head. "I'm here about my job. After the break you gave me, I wanted to give you plenty of notice. I've enrolled in classes and I'll be starting work in the university canteen closer to the time. If you don't mind, I'd like to stay on till then. I found a small place to rent and, frankly, I need the money."

The apartment wasn't much more than a room with a tiny bath attached. But it was affordable and clean and, most importantly, all hers.

"Of course you can stay on as long as you need to," Natalie said. "And I'm so pleased for you about the classes. But I do wish you'd let Alex have a word with Mateo."

Bailey found her feet. "It wouldn't work. Even if we got back together, he'd always wonder about my true feelings. Whether or not I'm a fraud." And, right or wrong, she didn't think she could ever get over the anger and disappointment that consumed her whenever she thought of his mistrust. "Still, I hope he finds someone who can make him happy."

Natalie sighed. "Alex and I thought he had."

The two women hugged and promised to keep in touch after Bailey handed in her notice. She was on her way out when she remembered to ask, "Did you and Alex come to a decision about Reece's shots?"

"We're going to take him in next week."

Bailey smiled. "I'm sure he'll be fine."

As she made her way to the bus stop, she rolled over in her mind their conversation. Given Mateo had gone so far as to buy her that ring, Natalie seemed convinced that he loved her. Bailey hadn't confessed that he'd barely batted an eye when she'd admitted that *she* loved *him*. Then again, given his doubtful nature—his ill-fated affair—he would only think she'd been playing her trump card to keep her foot in his door and her body in his bed.

Cringing, she walked faster.

She may not be a virgin but she would only ever sleep with a man if she wanted to share that most intimate part of herself with him. She hadn't been prepared to do that with Emilio, not that Mateo needed to know. The truly sad part was that she'd been burned enough by her Italian episode. Once bitten... Now, like Mateo, she couldn't imagine trusting anyone that much again. To know that he believed she would barter sex for a well-to-do lifestyle—that what they'd shared was essentially a lie—made her want to give up on relationships altogether.

As she neared the bus stop, a tall, suited figure stepped out from behind the shelter. When she recognized the height, the profile, every drop of blood froze in her veins. She was ready to turn straight around and walk away. She didn't want to see him. Didn't need to talk. But another, more resilient part propelled her on at the same time as that man came forward too.

She was shaking inside, but that didn't stop her from standing tall when she pulled up before him.

"What are you doing here? How did you know where to find me?"

"Since you left that morning after our argument," her father said, "I've kept track of your movements. I was about to take a deep breath and knock on your Mateo's front door before I saw you storm out. I contacted Mateo. He explained you two had had a falling out, and he told me which agency you worked for. The lady at the desk explained you were on their books to clean properties. I've waited around every day since, working through what I'd say when I saw you next."

Bailey swallowed against the emotion rising in her throat. "What did you come up with?"

"I don't know if she ever told you," Damon Ross said in a thick, graveled voice, "but your mother and I chose that bracelet together."

She wanted to clamp her hands over her ears. Instead she held them up. "I'm done fighting over that."

"I wanted to get you a gold pin with your name on it," he went on. "But, like always," his smile was both sad and fond, "Ann had her way. And, I'll give it to her, usually she was right. But not always." In his pristine jacket, his shoulders stooped. "Sometimes she was dead wrong."

Bailey's chest ached so badly she didn't want to take another breath. Her father had never opened up like this before. As if he genuinely wanted to help her understand. Still, that lesser part of her whispered in her ear. *Walk away. Say something that will hurt him for a change.* But she couldn't. When everything was said and done, he was her father and he was reaching out. But she needed to make him understand too.

"I know you miss her," she said, "but, Dad, I miss her, too."

He nodded slowly as his gaze trailed off.

"I thought something was wrong," he admitted. "We can all have trouble remembering where we put the keys. We've all missed appointments. But when she couldn't coordinate your activities…when she forgot to pick you up from school…" His features hardened and he thrust out his chin. "I told her I was taking her for a checkup. Yes, she was a free spirit. That's what I loved about her most. She always wanted to do it her way. But just that once—"

He paused and air leaked from his chest before he went on.

"Just that once, I wish she'd have listened." His chin firmed up again. "I should have insisted. Taken her to the doctor myself instead of buttoning my lip when she insisted it was nothing."

Her throat clogged, Bailey's thoughts raced. She couldn't get her mind around what he was saying.

"You blame yourself for her stroke?"

"Sometimes…yes, I do. Her grandmother died of an aneurysm at a young age. Her own mother died of similar complications the year before she passed." His eyes met hers and he smiled. "You're so like her. So headstrong."

"Is that why you pushed me away?"

"Makes no sense to say it aloud but I didn't want to lose you too. I made a pact the day we buried your mother that no matter how much I might want to give in to you, you'd do as you were told. I was going to protect and guide you and I didn't care if you ended up hating me because of it."

"I never hated you." Her voice cracked. "I just couldn't understand why you were so…distant. When Mom was alive, everything seemed so simple." So warm and so safe. "When she died, it felt like the biggest part of me died with her. After the funeral I felt so alone. I got mixed up with the wrong crowd and dropped out because I didn't think anyone cared."

He closed his eyes for a moment as if wishing he could take all those hurt feelings away. "Every day since you left I told myself that I shouldn't be so hard on you. I should be happy to watch you grow, make your mistakes."

She admitted, "I made a few."

"Most of them because I wasn't there the way I should have been."

He fished into his suit jacket pocket. When his hand opened, the gold chain and charms shone out like the treasure that it was. His eyes glistened with unshed tears.

"This is yours."

He took her hand and laid the bracelet in her palm. She gazed down, remembering those happy childhood days—her mother and the father she'd loved so much—and her heart rolled over. Tears ready to fall, she rested her cheek on her father's shoulder and Damon Ross at last brought his daughter close.

Mateo downed the last of his scotch, set his glass on the clubhouse counter and gestured to the bartender. He needed another drink. Make that a double.

Beside him, Alex held up a hand. "No more for me. I told Nat I'd be home by six-thirty."

Mateo argued. "We only got off the course an hour ago."

"And I'm ready to gloat to my wife about how I beat you on both the front *and* back nine." Alex's mouth shifted to one side. "Not that you've been focused on anything much lately."

Two weeks had passed since Bailey had walked out. Admittedly, he'd been preoccupied. Mateo was gesturing to the bartender again.

"I'll be back at work soon."

"And you think that'll help?"

Mateo pretended not to hear that last comment. It was high time he got back to the practice. He was going crazy hanging around that big house. Nothing to do. Only ghosts to talk to. When he'd been with Bailey he'd been happy to postpone visiting Mama. Since she'd gone, he'd considered flying to Italy to fill in the time more than anything, but he knew if he happened upon Emilio he might just punch him in the nose.

"Why don't you come back and have dinner at home with us," Alex said. "Natalie would love to see you. Reece too. I told you he had his shots earlier this week."

"A couple of times. I'm glad there weren't any serious side-effects."

Alex raised his brows. "You're not the only one. So, what about dinner?"

"Thanks. I'll have something here."

Mateo collected his fresh glass while Alex asked to settle his tab.

As Alex brought the leather booklet closer and looked over the items, he asked, "Ever heard the saying, love never comes easy?"

"I'm not in the mood for a lecture." Mateo swirled his ice.

"What about some sound words from a friend then?"

"She's gone, Alex." Mateo took a long sip. Swallowed and enjoyed the burn. "No happily ever afters here."

Alex signed and waited for the bartender to leave before he thatched his hands on the timber counter and asked, "Why do you hold on to it so fiercely?"

"Hold on to what?"

"You're not losing anything by admitting you love her."

"You know, you're right." Mateo found his feet. "Time to go."

"To that great big empty house," Alex reminded him,

following out of the crowded room filled with nineteenth hole chatter.

At the exit, Mateo stopped and rotated around. "I let Bailey know I thought she was a con."

Alex shrugged. "You were wrong."

"Yeah. I was wrong."

He'd let Bailey walk away that day two weeks ago, telling himself he had no choice. He was protecting himself. Doing the right thing. But he'd printed off that email and as the hours and then days passed, he read it over again and again. Bailey had insisted that her dialogue in that email had been that of a woman in love. In love with him. He hadn't wanted to listen. Even when his heart wanted to believe it, his brain didn't want to take the risk. Because this kind of decision was only the beginning. When you were a couple, you had to tend the garden every day, do everything you could to make certain the union survived. And if it didn't...if the marriage failed and you had kids...

Mateo headed for the cab stand.

Better that things had turned out the way they did.

Alex was on his tail. The sun was lying low, getting ready to set. The air was muggy. Stifling. Mateo was a whisker from ripping off his shirt.

"So admit it."

Mateo looked at Alex, striding beside him. "Admit what?"

"That you were wrong."

"Just did."

"To *her*."

"Sure. I suppose I could kick it off with something like... 'Hey, Bailey, I was wondering if you could ever forgive me for being the world's biggest jerk.'"

Alex tugged his ear. "That's a start."

Mateo confessed, "I found that message and—" What felt

like a sharpened pencil drove into his temple. Growling, he waved off the rest. "Ah, forget it."

But Alex wasn't letting him off. "And what?"

Mateo stopped and studied his feet. His heart.

"And suddenly…I felt as if I had nothing. Was nothing. It's weird. I have so much. Too damn much. But where it counts…" He shut his eyes. *Oh God.* "I'm empty."

"You don't have to be."

Mateo's jaw shifted as his stomach sank more. "I never knew my biological parents."

Alex rested his hand on his friend's shoulder. "You'd make a great father."

"Bailey said that to me once."

"She's a wise lady."

"And I'm a jackass."

"Not usually but in this instance…"

Mateo looked over. Alex was grinning.

He would've liked to smile back but he shrugged instead. "How do I fix this? What on earth do I say?"

"The sixty-four million dollar question." Alex flagged down a cab. "The truth is always a good place to start."

Seventeen

"Just shout if it's a bad time to drop in."

Knowing that voice, feeling her heart instantly crash against her ribs, Bailey gathered herself in record time and turned to face her attractive, uninvited guest.

"Okay," she said, devoid of emotion. "It's a bad time to drop in."

She angled back to climb her building's first flight of stairs. Mateo Celeca was right there beside her, his arms out, offering to carry her grocery bags.

"I'll help with those," he said.

Ignoring him, she kept climbing.

"Nice complex," he said when they reached the first landing.

She leveled him a glare—*Go away!*—and went on walking.

"Nat said you handed in notice at the real estate agency," he said.

She groaned and kept walking. "Whatever it is you've come to say, please, just say it."

"I thought we could catch a coffee some place."

"Thank you. No."

She tackled the last of the stairs and crossed to her apartment's front door.

"Bailey, I want to say I'm sorry."

His words hit her so hard she lost her breath. But apologies didn't make a difference in how she felt. She bolstered her resolve.

"Terrific." She placed her bags on the ground, found her key and fit it in the lock. "Goodbye."

"Also, I need to mention I was an idiot. I made assumptions and I shouldn't have."

She bent to retrieve the bags, but he'd collected them and was already moving around her and inside. Her tongue burned to let loose and tell him to get out before she called security. But why not let him see how she lived now? He might need all his "stuff" but she certainly did not. Cozy suited her just fine.

"A bit different from what you're used to," she said as he slid the bags on the modest kitchenette counter.

His brows knitted, he cast a glance around. "It's, ah, very clean."

Then, as if she'd invited him to stay, he pulled out a stool. Not happening. Since speaking with her father—making amends there—she'd progressed by leaps and bounds this last week. New place, new job and new life on the way. She wasn't prepared to take a backward step now. She would not let her past feelings for Mateo hoodwink her into thinking for a moment "this" was anything other than over.

"I understand you must feel bad about what you said and even worse about how you acted. You should. But you've said

sorry. Hell, I'll even accept the apology. Now," she fanned the
door open, "have a nice life."

Not quite a smile, his mouth tugged to one side. "You don't
mean that."

"Actually, I don't. But *I wish you nothing but happiness*
would've been even harder to believe."

A muscle leapt to life in his cheek as he pushed to his feet.
By the time he'd strolled over, Bailey's pulse had climbed so
high, she swore it hit a bell. But he didn't sweep her up into
his arms and carry her away. He didn't even try to crowd her
back against the wall and kiss her. He merely closed the door,
then gestured for her to take a seat.

Holding her ground, Bailey crossed her arms.

"It's over, Mateo. I can spell it out for you if you like, but
other than that, if you don't mind I have things to—"

She'd reached to turn the door handle. In an instant, his
hot hand had covered hers and her gaze jumped to his, his
face set and passionate. God help her, he'd never looked more
handsome.

"Bailey, what we shared is a long way from over."

Wrenching back, she moved well away. She didn't need to
get that close to him. Didn't need to smell his musky scent.
Feel that animal heat.

"Do you think that little of me?" She asked. "*Turn on
the charm and she'll forget how I suggested she could be
bought.* Dr. Celeca, you could be the richest, most powerful,
best looking man in the world and it wouldn't make a scrap
of difference as to how I feel about you now."

"I understand."

She looked at him sideways then blinked.

"Well…*good.*"

"From the moment we met," he said, "I made assumptions.
I was hard on you, suspicious. Not because of Mama and

Emilio. I'm sure I believed you on both counts near to the start."

"So you made me feel like a felon because it rains on Tuesdays?"

A smile curved his lips as he prowled two steps nearer.

"I was hard on you because you made me look at myself. Not the doctor or investor or benefactor. At the *stripped down* me with absolutely nothing to hide behind. And, *Dio buono,* that scared me like you wouldn't believe."

Breathing shallow, she rotated away. *I don't want to hear this. It won't make a difference.*

"Before I met you," he went on, "I knew what I wanted. Success. Security. If I had somewhere solid where I felt I belonged, I had everything I needed. But all the possessions in the world could never be enough because what I need can't be bought."

She shrugged. "Take a bow."

An arm wound around her waist but not firmly enough. She maneuvered out and held up both hands.

"This has gone on long enough. I'd like to say we could be friends but—"

"Dammit, Bailey, I want more than your friendship."

He hadn't raised his voice but something in the timbre set her nerves jangling and her blood racing even faster.

"I know what you want," she said. "But I'm happy the way I am. There are goals I want to accomplish and I want to achieve them my way."

"There's no room for *our* way?" he asked.

She thought of her father's admission—of how her mother hadn't wanted his help when she'd needed it most—and a sliver of doubt pierced her armor.

"I've thought long and hard about this," Mateo said, coming close again. "The way I see it, this is about trust. I needed to trust you. Now you need to trust me."

She huffed and stepped back. "Sorry. Tried that."

"And I let you down."

"Damn right you did."

"But love is about forgiveness."

"No one mentioned *love*." At least he hadn't.

"I have something for you."

She lifted her brows at his change of subject. She guessed what his something was.

"I'm not interested in your big diamond ring, Mateo."

"It's not a ring. I only hope you like it enough." He reached into his trouser pocket and retrieved something small and gold.

Bailey's heart pounded as she gazed down at the Eiffel Tower trinket nestled in the palm of his hand. She couldn't help it. Her eyes misted over and she suddenly felt so weak... so *vulnerable*.

"France was only a week out of our lives."

"The most important week," he said. "The week we fell in love. I love you, Bailey. You loved me then. I'm here because I need to know...do you love me still?"

She searched his eyes...searched her heart. The truth wasn't that simple.

"I don't know," she said.

"Because I made a mistake." Before she could answer, he went on. "An unbelievably huge mistake." Pressing her lips together, she nodded. "Your father made mistakes too. You've made mistakes."

"I don't know that I can forgive you that one."

"I understand." He stepped nearer. "I do." His palm trailed her cheek, her chin. "I'd do anything to take it back."

She closed her eyes to shut out the bitter sting and ache of emotion. "I never wanted your money."

"I always wanted you." A light kiss dropped on the side

of her mouth. "Marry me, Bailey. Be my wife. I need you in my life and you need me. Every day. Every night."

"Because you love me."

He groaned against her lips. "So much."

"And because..."

His hand covered hers and the charm. "Because...?"

Overcome with emotion, finally beaten and glad of it, she gazed into his eyes and admitted.

"Because I love you."

His eyes flashed a heartbeat before his mouth lowered and captured hers.

She was helpless to deny the pleasure, couldn't stop herself from pressing in. As one palm cradled the back of her head and his steaming hard body curled over hers, Bailey could only cling to his shoulder, grateful tears squeezing from her eyes, heart filled to overflowing.

When his lips reluctantly left hers, her head was spinning. But his smile, so close, and his hands, so warm, left her wonderfully anchored.

"Marry me," he whispered.

Another tear slid down her cheek as she took a breath and surrendered. "Yes, Mateo," she murmured. "I'll marry you. I want to be your wife."

A tingling wave of desire and contentment spiraled through her as the man she couldn't help but adore—the soul mate she couldn't help but trust in—kissed her once more. Bailey held on, smiling...belonging...believing...

All the world lay in the palm of their hands.

Epilogue

Mateo had decided this should be a surprise. Bailey argued; everyone liked to be given at least some notice before guests drop by. When he pulled up outside Ville Laube's Chapelle and Madame Garnier's face lit with amazement, then a group of children edged forward, he laughed and, leaning over, snatched a kiss from his beautiful bride's cheek.

"You see," he said. "Sometimes it's good to be caught off guard."

"I know someone who's going to be a little more than that."

But they'd already agreed. Mateo would give Remy his gift in private. There were other bombshells to drop first.

As the new Dr. and Mrs. Celeca moved forward and the crowd of kids grew larger, someone in the tower rang the bell. Nichole Garnier was one of the first to meet them. Holding her face, she looked lost for words.

Mateo kissed both Madame's cheeks.

"I don't understand," Nichole started. "We only said goodbye. How long are you staying?"

"A while." He and Bailey shared a look. *A long while.*

Mateo was about to explain when he caught sight of Remy, standing by the side, one mitten cupping his brow.

"Remy!" Mateo called out. "Come say hello."

By now children were racing around them, hugging their guests' legs and singing as if school was out for a year.

Laughing too, Madame demanded to know. "Tell me! What are you doing here?"

"Bailey and I have decided to move to France permanently. There's still a mountain of forms to fill out and sign, but—"

"Mon dieu." Madame interrupted. *"Here?"*

"Actually, over there."

When he waved toward his cottage, Nichole failed to catch her yelp of delight.

Clairdy was there dancing around, first like a ballerina then a break dancer. Laughing, Bailey crouched down beside her little friend. "Do you understand, Clairdy?"

Nichole ran a hand over the little girl's head and spoke in French. Up to speed now, Clairdy's eyes sparkled before she cartwheeled away and back again. She was telling the other children. *Monsieur and Mademoiselle are married and living here with us!*

Remy must have heard; he came running up, full speed. Mateo bent to catch his hare. The momentum swung them both halfway around. After the commotion settled enough, Mateo drew Remy away, out of others' earshot.

"I have some other news, Remy." He held the boy's hand and continued to speak in French. "Bailey and I would like you to live with us."

But Remy didn't react the way Mateo had hoped. His face filled with uncertainty and his wide eyes darted first right then left. Frowning, Mateo shifted. He hadn't explained properly.

"Remy, if you want me to be your father..." He inhaled deeply and said the words he'd held back for too long. "I'd like you to be my son."

But the boy's expression furrowed more. He looked as if he'd been given the biggest gift under the tree but for some reason couldn't open it.

With a knuckle, Mateo gently tipped up his chin. "What's wrong?"

"Monsieur, I cannot go." The boy held a hand out to where his friend stood dancing with the others. "I cannot leave Clairdy behind."

"You want Clairdy to come with us?" Mateo smiled. "To be your sister?"

"She will be good," Remy promised. "She won't talk too much. I'll tell her."

Mateo chuckled. "We've already thought about your Clairdy. If she'd like to join our little family, we'd love to have her."

Remy gave a *yip!* then raced off to tell Clairdy the good news while Mateo raveled his wonderful wife into his arms.

"I'm thinking we need a dog. How about a Labradoodle?"

Bailey wrapped her arms around his neck and stole a kiss. "You remembered?"

"Why don't we name him after your father?"

"Damon the Labradoodle?" She nodded. "I like it. He can keep you and Remy company while you work on the cottage."

"Yes. Another couple of rooms."

"A cubbyhouse out back."

Letting out a breath, he took in his surroundings...the majesty of the Chapelle surround by a pile of noisy children. "How strange that I should end up back here."

"I think it's perfect. Well, *almost* perfect." She stroked his cheek and spoke earnestly. "Mateo, now I have a surprise for you."

She tilted her chin over his shoulder.

A man was walking up and for a moment Mateo thought he knew him...the hawkish nose, those kind, light gray eyes. Something unique about the way he walked. Mateo's mind wound back, further and faster. Absently he touched the scar on one side of his lip then shook his head slowly.

It couldn't be.

The name came out a threadbare croak.

"Henri?"

Upon him now, the man hugged him tight and then Mateo knew for certain. His childhood friend who had left all those years ago. Mateo never thought they'd see each other again.

"You are the same," Henri said, laughing and clapping Mateo's shoulder.

Beaming, Mateo brushed the top of Henri's head. "You're taller!"

Henri's gaze hooked onto Bailey, her hands clasped under her chin. He exclaimed, "This is the lady we have to thank for finding and bringing us here."

Mateo pinned Bailey with a curious look.

You did this?

Looking set to burst, she nodded. Now Mateo was the one lost for words.

"I hear you're married, Mateo. And after marriage," Henri said, "comes children. I'm afraid you have some catching up to do." Henri stepped aside. A woman with three children stood behind him. "My wife, Talli. These three rascals belong to us."

The rascals, introduced as Mimi, Luc and Andre, asked if they could play then ran off to join in the other children's games while Nichole rushed inside to have more settings placed for lunch. While Talli and Bailey chatted, Mateo and Henri caught up. Henri lived many miles from the Chapelle. His adoptive father had died and his adoptive mother married again. Change of name, a few changes of address. It made sense that Mateo's search for him had come up empty.

"Until Nichole and your beautiful wife put their heads together. They left no stone unturned."

Mateo explained about Ernesto, his move to Australia and how he'd decided to give up his practice there to live and enjoy a simpler life here.

When Nichole called everyone in for lunch, Mateo held Bailey back.

"I have never been so surprised," he told her as he brought her close and searched her adoring eyes. "Thank you." And then he kissed her with all that his body and soul could give.

When their lips softly parted, he kept her near. He couldn't put into words how much he loved her. How her love had saved him.

Smiling, he shrugged. "You have given me *everything*."

Bailey's heart glistened in her eyes as she replied in French, "Then, *mon amour,* we are even."

* * * * *

Harlequin® Desire

COMING NEXT MONTH
Available July 12, 2011

#2095 CAUGHT IN THE BILLIONAIRE'S EMBRACE
Elizabeth Bevarly

#2096 ONE NIGHT, TWO HEIRS
Maureen Child
Texas Cattleman's Club: The Showdown

#2097 THE TYCOON'S TEMPORARY BABY
Emily McKay
Billionaires and Babies

#2098 A LONE STAR LOVE AFFAIR
Sara Orwig
Stetsons & CEOs

#2099 ONE MONTH WITH THE MAGNATE
Michelle Celmer
Black Gold Billionaires

#2100 FALLING FOR THE PRINCESS
Sandra Hyatt

You can find more information on upcoming
Harlequin® titles, free excerpts and more at
www.HarlequinInsideRomance.com.

REQUEST YOUR FREE BOOKS!
2 FREE NOVELS PLUS 2 FREE GIFTS!

ALWAYS POWERFUL, PASSIONATE AND PROVOCATIVE

YES! Please send me 2 FREE Harlequin Desire® novels and my 2 FREE gifts (gifts are worth about $10). After receiving them, if I don't wish to receive any more books, I can return the shipping statement marked "cancel." If I don't cancel, I will receive 6 brand-new novels every month and be billed just $4.05 per book in the U.S. or $4.74 per book in Canada. That's a saving of at least 15% off the cover price! It's quite a bargain! Shipping and handling is just 50¢ per book in the U.S. and 75¢ per book in Canada.* I understand that accepting the 2 free books and gifts places me under no obligation to buy anything. I can always return a shipment and cancel at any time. Even if I never buy another book, the two free books and gifts are mine to keep forever.

225/326 SDN FC65

Name	(PLEASE PRINT)	
Address		Apt. #
City	State/Prov.	Zip/Postal Code

Signature (if under 18, a parent or guardian must sign)

Mail to the **Reader Service:**
IN U.S.A.: P.O. Box 1867, Buffalo, NY 14240-1867
IN CANADA: P.O. Box 609, Fort Erie, Ontario L2A 5X3

Not valid for current subscribers to Harlequin Desire books.

Want to try two free books from another line?
Call 1-800-873-8635 or visit www.ReaderService.com.

* Terms and prices subject to change without notice. Prices do not include applicable taxes. Sales tax applicable in N.Y. Canadian residents will be charged applicable taxes. Offer not valid in Quebec. This offer is limited to one order per household. All orders subject to credit approval. Credit or debit balances in a customer's account(s) may be offset by any other outstanding balance owed by or to the customer. Please allow 4 to 6 weeks for delivery. Offer available while quantities last.

Your Privacy—The Reader Service is committed to protecting your privacy. Our Privacy Policy is available online at www.ReaderService.com or upon request from the Reader Service.

We make a portion of our mailing list available to reputable third parties that offer products we believe may interest you. If you prefer that we not exchange your name with third parties, or if you wish to clarify or modify your communication preferences, please visit us at www.ReaderService.com/consumerschoice or write to us at Reader Service Preference Service, P.O. Box 9062, Buffalo, NY 14269. Include your complete name and address.

HDES11

USA TODAY *bestselling author B.J. Daniels*
takes you on a trip to Whitehorse, Montana,
and the Chisholm Cattle Company.

RUSTLED

Available July 2011 from Harlequin Intrigue.

As the dust settled, Dawson got his first good look at the rustler. A pair of big Montana sky-blue eyes glared up at him from a face framed by blond curls.

A woman rustler?

"You have to let me go," she hollered as the roar of the stampeding cattle died off in the distance.

"So you can finish stealing my cattle? I don't think so." Dawson jerked the woman to her feet.

She reached for the gun strapped to her hip hidden under her long barn jacket.

He grabbed the weapon before she could, his eyes narrowing as he assessed her. "How many others are there?" he demanded, grabbing a fistful of her jacket. "I think you'd better start talking before I tear into you."

She tried to fight him off, but he was on to her tricks and pinned her to the ground. He was suddenly aware of the soft curves beneath the jean jacket she wore under her coat.

"You have to listen to me." She ground out the words from between her gritted teeth. "You have to let me go. If you don't they will come back for me and they will kill you. There are too many of them for you to fight off alone. You won't stand a chance and I don't want your blood on my hands."

"I'm touched by your concern for me. Especially after you just tried to pull a gun on me."

"I wasn't going to shoot you."

Dawson hauled her to her feet and walked her the rest of the way to his horse. Reaching into his saddlebag, he pulled out a length of rope.

"You can't tie me up."

He pulled her hands behind her back and began to tie her wrists together.

"If you let me go, I can keep them from coming back," she said. "You have my word." She let out an unladylike curse. "I'm just trying to save your sorry neck."

"And I'm just going after my cattle."

"Don't you mean your boss's cattle?"

"Those cattle are mine."

"*You're* a Chisholm?"

"Dawson Chisholm. And you are…?"

"Everyone calls me Jinx."

He chuckled. "I can see why."

Bronco busting, falling in love…it's all in a day's work.
Look for the rest of their story in

RUSTLED

Available July 2011 from Harlequin Intrigue
wherever books are sold.